PROMETHEUS RESCUE

STAR STREAKER #4

T.M. CATRON

ANTIMATTER BOOKS

For Dad
who made me a lifelong reader

CHAPTER ONE

A NARROW STREET meandered through the eastern portion of the city, branching off like the limbs of a gnarled tree. Bright green ivy from Old Earth thrived in the yellow sunlight that glowed with the brilliance of liquid gold. It was midday for the planet Ares. A large merchant ship drifted across the sun, casting a momentary shadow over the street before fading away on its journey into space.

Captain Rance Cooper watched the ship with a twinge of jealousy. At least the large, clunky freighter had cargo—cargo it was being paid to carry. Rance and her crew had spent the last two months in hiding without a job, and without the money that came with it. They'd already spent more time on Ares than she'd planned, and Rance was becoming impatient at their self-imposed seclusion.

She sighed and focused on the marketplace around her. Vendors' stalls made of poles and brightly colored fabrics crowded both sides of the road, leaving a narrow walkway down the center. The flags didn't flutter in the close, still air, but the warm smell of yeast bread floated along the street, causing Rance's mouth to water. It wasn't the kind of bread that had to be rehydrated, either, but freshly baked goodness straight from an oven.

Rance's stomach grumbled, and she paused to look at the purple and yellow water vegetables Ares was famous for growing—vagrappes. They looked like squids with no heads, with long roots protruding out of both ends like long, squishy tentacles. At the back of the stall, older, slightly rotten vegetables were heaped together for bargain prices. What would the crew say if she came back to the ship with wilted vegetables?

Irritated that she had such limited options for feeding her crew, Rance wound her long braid around her hand. Realizing what she was doing, she dropped her braid and sighed.

On the opposite side of the stall, a dark-haired boy of about eight ran a dirty hand over the vegetables. The merchant shooed him away. The boy scampered off down the street, revealing torn, dirty clothes, skinny arms, and bony knees sticking out from his too-short tunic.

As Rance watched him go, she spotted something that made her stomach growl even louder. Two stalls down, a merchant sold lantess from the deep river nearby. The monster fish had four fins, a long tail, and beautiful silver scales covering its body. Lantess were delicacies across the galaxy. Rance had grown up eating them on Xanthes, but only on special occasions. The sight of the fish made her drool in vain. Even here, lantess were ridiculously expensive. With only fifty credits to split between a crew of six, the captain had to spend her money wisely. And fifty credits wasn't enough money to purchase an eyeball, let alone a whole fish.

Two months on Ares had forced the crew to tighten their belts. Rance had taken local jobs, transporting goods back and forth between the planets of the system. But they hadn't ventured further beyond it—her father, Davos, would still be looking for her.

And Unity, the military arm of the Empire Triton, would still be looking for Solaris. But Triton couldn't police the entire Galaxy—not yet. Since arriving on Ares, Solaris had stood directly beneath a large picture of his face projected onto the city's holograms.

No one had noticed. The planets of the Outer Colonies had a more relaxed military presence than the Core Worlds.

Eventually, Unity had even stopped broadcasting Solaris' face all over official channels. He insisted that they hadn't given up and were merely rethinking their strategy. He could change his face at will, after all. How would they catch a man like that?

Rance stared at the lantess. The last time she'd eaten it, she'd been sitting in her home on Xanthes, listening to her father drone on about her betrothal to Harrison McConnell. Seeing the fish should have made her gag from the memory, but she was hungry enough to forget that particular unpleasantness associated with the fish.

Then, she had an idea.

"Excuse me, sir," Rance asked the merchant.

He turned. The merchant was a skinny, weathered-looking man with leathery skin and squinty eyes—the appearance of one who spent days out on the river, catching a food source he couldn't afford to eat himself.

"Ah," he said, gesturing to his fish. "Does the captain wish to buy today?"

"No, thank you, but I have a question. Do you need to send any lantess out of the system? I have a ship."

"Ah. Alas, I wish to know if your ship is big?"

Rance tried to hide the sigh that threatened to slip through her lips. "It's small, but maybe you need a special delivery somewhere?"

"Ah." He shook his head and smiled. "I only make big deliveries."

The merchant spread his arms wide and smiled.

Oh well. Rance hadn't been eager to stink up the cargo bay of the *Star Streaker* with fish, anyway. But she was hungry enough to do it.

"Ah. Do you wish to buy?" he asked again.

Rance shook her head. "Not today."

She moved on down the street, trying to forget about the sweet, salty taste of lantess or the ache in her stomach.

Whether Unity was still looking for them or not, the crew didn't have a choice but to find a job soon—a good job. They'd starve to death otherwise, or be forced to sell the ship, and Rance would sooner cut off her own arm and eat it for breakfast than lose the *Streaker*.

Ahead of her, Solaris walked down the street from the opposite direction. His face and hair were dark—different from his customary pale skin and shaggy brown hair. To blend in with the local population, he wore a brown shirt and loose slacks instead of the crew's navy flight suit. Rance recognized him, anyway. Since meeting the Galaxy Wizard two months earlier, she had learned to recognize Solaris' tall, lean body and confident bearing whether she knew his face or not.

He was empty-handed. Apparently, the food didn't get any cheaper farther down. Solaris saw her and nodded to the fish.

"Maybe we can rent a boat with our credits and catch some lantess for ourselves."

Rance frowned. "James would probably fall into the water, and we'd have to pluck him from the jaws of a man-eating lantess."

Lantess were famously dangerous. If provoked, one live fish could shred a man to the bone with its wide mouth and razor-sharp teeth.

"Really? James?" Solaris asked in surprise. "He's not a bumbling idiot."

"You've never seen him try to swim. James is a great pilot—skillful, confident—"

"A bit over-confident."

"—fearless. Great qualities when we're running from Unity Dark Fighters or angry pirates. In water, he sinks like a star being sucked into a black hole."

"It's just as well," Solaris said ruefully. "Ares' fishing industry is protected by local thugs who are paid by big fishing corporations. They brutally guard their territories with heavy weaponry, armored mercenaries, and a tendency to throw would-be fishermen to the lantess."

"No fishing, then."

"No. Guess not."

"Why did you suggest it?"

"I'm hungry."

Solaris wandered away toward another stall and asked

the merchant about his prices. Rance began searching for the seller of the bread she'd smelled earlier.

Maybe she should beg for food.

Rance had never begged for anything in her life. She wasn't that desperate yet, was she?

After a moment of deliberation, the captain decided she was too hungry to care what anybody thought. But begging wasn't an option, either. Rance's position aboard the ship wasn't a secret. No one in his right mind would believe that the tall, composed captain of the *Star Streaker* couldn't afford her own supper. She sighed.

After two months, the *Streaker* still attracted attention. Passersby gawked in amazement like a bronze statue had been placed on the landing pad. It sort of had. Except for two small runs, the ship had baked in the sunshine of Ares day after day, serving no purpose other than to provide a home for Rance and her crew.

What a failure she'd turned out to be.

Before Rance could sink deeper into her misery, a commotion upset the quiet, orderly marketplace and interrupted her self-pity. Buyers shifted out of the way as the dark-haired boy she'd seen earlier sprinted down the street. The vegetable seller ran after him like a dog chasing a rabbit.

The boy's arms overflowed with purple tubers. They flew out of his arms as he crashed into the crowd and maneuvered around the stalls. The faster he ran, the more vagrappes tumbled to the ground.

The chase had almost reached Solaris, who was watching with interest. The merchant's hand reached out to grab the boy's tunic, but the boy narrowly dodged him. Then, the kid took advantage of an opening between two fishermen, and the chase headed right for Solaris.

She half-wished Solaris would stick out his foot to trip the merchant.

Instead, Solaris reached out and grabbed the boy by the arm.

Rance cringed. Apparently, her CO couldn't forget twenty years of upholding the law. Why couldn't he just let the boy run away? She hurried over. The last thing they needed was to draw attention to themselves.

The kid wriggled and kicked at Solaris' shins. But Solaris' long arm held the boy's feet well out of range. The merchant arrived, panting and red-faced. Without pausing for breath, he began shouting. The boy cringed and tried to pull away. The last of the vegetables fell out of his arms, except a lone tuber that he clutched firmly between his shaking hands.

Solaris kept his grip firm. "Give it up, lad."

"The boy must be turned over to the authorities!" the merchant said, pulling a communicator from his robes. "He's ruined my vagrappes!"

"Wait," Solaris said. "I'm sure he'll pick them up and return them."

The man's face turned three shades redder. "I don't want them returned! He's touched them with his grubby hands! There's no telling what diseases he carries."

"He's just hungry," Rance said, coming up beside them.

The merchant glared at her. "Then he should pay for them like everybody else!"

"He obviously can't pay for them," Solaris said, his own face growing red. "Or he would have done so."

"You Core Worlders don't know anything about life on

Ares. He can pay for them. He can work like everybody else and pay like everybody else. Instead, he chooses to steal for a living."

"Yes, because he looks like he does so well at that!" Rance snapped. "Look at him. He's starving!"

With the three adults towering over him, the boy's eyes widened in fear. He still gripped the vagrappe like his life depended on it. Maybe it did.

"There's no need to call the authorities," Solaris said, his voice growing cold with anger. "He's been frightened enough."

"Hmph. He needs to be taught a lesson." The merchant grabbed for the boy, but Solaris let go of the kid and stepped between them. Seizing his chance, the boy scurried away with his one lonely vegetable.

A vein bulged in the merchant's forehead. "You idiot. You let him get away!"

A crowd had gathered, encircling Solaris, Rance, and the furious merchant in what was clearly the day's entertainment.

Rance thought the man's attitude was disgusting, but she held back from telling him exactly what she thought. They had already drawn too much attention.

"We'll pay for it," Rance said, desperate to get out of the limelight.

"The *boy* must pay! He stole! I work hard to support my family, and he has spit all over our living."

"He did no such thing!" Solaris said. "We are offering to pay for the vagrappe in his stead."

The man sniffed and fixed them with a cold stare. "All of them."

"All?"

"Yes. You will pay for *all* the vagrappes he ruined, or I will call the authorities now."

Solaris stood up straight, using his superior height to tower over the man. "What do you charge?"

"Fifty credits."

"Fifty?" Rance choked out. That was all they had left. All she had left in the world—unless she wanted to siphon fuel from the *Star Streaker*. Without fuel, she might as well sell the ship.

"We'll pay it," Solaris said.

He pulled out his handset and transferred the funds to the merchant. Rance shook her head. If Solaris had just let the boy run by in the first place, they wouldn't have just lost their ability to buy dinner for the crew.

Even though Rance was annoyed, buying dinner would only have delayed the inevitable. They needed to leave Ares and find a real job. She repeated this fact to herself as the merchant stormed off, mumbling about *interfering off-worlders.*

She looked around at the dispersing crowd, many of them frowning and clearly disappointed the argument hadn't escalated to something more exciting.

Solaris spun around to Rance. "Why did you get involved? Don't think I can handle it?"

Rance gaped at him, shocked that he was mad at *her*. "Oh yes, you handled that spectacularly. Why didn't you let the kid run by? He was just hungry, *Roote*," she said, using Solaris' alias. They always used it in public.

"Being hungry doesn't give him the right to steal."

"And being poor doesn't mean he deserves to starve!"

"Says the woman who's never been poor in her life."

Angry heat rose to Rance's face, dampening her ability to control her temper. "I'm feeling pretty poor right now since we just paid our last fifty credits for *one* vagrappe."

"No, *eight* vagrappes. And you're the one who suggested we pay for them!"

"Only because you turned into a law-abiding citizen all of a sudden!"

She squared off with Solaris, daring him to say something else stupid so they could continue the fight. But he didn't, so they silently fumed in the middle of the street, glaring at each other while foot traffic made a wide berth around them.

The argument was inevitable, the result of two months of inactivity. Small rations and little work had made the crew snippy with one another. Rance and Solaris had not been immune to the struggle, but they had held off at actually shouting at each other.

Until now.

"We've got to find work anyway," Solaris said, shooting Rance a dirty look before breaking the staring contest. "We could stay on Ares and debate it until the river dries up, but eventually we just have to leave and see what happens."

Despite Solaris' practical advice, they continued to argue all the way to the *Star Streaker*. Rance was cross at Solaris for interfering with the boy. Solaris was angry at Rance for interfering with *him*. When he blamed her for losing the fifty credits, she'd had enough.

"Just forget it," she said. "That's an order. We're getting off this rock."

Solaris closed his mouth, but she imagined he was silently continuing his rant all the way across the landing pad. The expression on his face left little doubt about his thoughts.

The sight of the *Star Streaker* improved Rance's mood only a little. The streamlined, bronze space cruiser gleamed, and the setting sun sent just the right angle of light bouncing off the cockpit window.

Rance's chest swelled with pride, and she sighed with relief at seeing her home. Their situation wasn't as bad as she made it out to be. They had the *Streaker* and the best crew in the galaxy. If that didn't count for something, nothing did.

Solaris wasn't experiencing the same fuzzy feelings, however. As they entered the cargo bay, he sniffed in annoyance.

"Got a problem?" Rance asked with as much snark as she could muster.

"You're so naive, Rance Cooper."

"And you're a tiresome know-it-all, Solaris."

He nodded in infuriating acknowledgment as they climbed the ramp into the cargo bay. Inside, dark metal had been polished until it gleamed like the outside. The floor was spotless—it should have been, considering it hadn't been used lately. The very air of the ship screamed luxury even down to the smooth door leading to the engine room. Luxury and cleanliness.

At least if they starved, they'd do it in style.

A warm glow shone out from the galley. Harper, upon hearing Rance and Solaris' voices, peeked her head around the door. Her shock of straight, dark hair stuck up wildly. Her usual bangs fell into her eyes.

Embarrassed that she hadn't brought dinner, Rance avoided Harper's eye as she walked into the galley.

But the tiny science officer didn't heap guilt on them when she saw the captain's empty hands. "Are we going to take on a job, then, Captain?" she asked.

Harper's soft voice and warm nature fooled strangers into thinking she was a simple young woman. But she was sharp, and her abilities went far beyond the duties she performed on the *Star Streaker*. She could have had a job performing advanced hyperspace calculations onboard a Unity ship, or on one of the private runners that ferried nobles from planet to planet. But Harper preferred the quiet life onboard the *Streaker* and maintaining the ship's new AI, Deliverance.

Okay, maybe life onboard the *Streaker* wasn't that quiet, Rance thought. Only the last two months had been quiet. Ever since they had returned from the disaster on Coru where they'd narrowly avoided some murderous thugs.

"Sorry, Harper," Rance said. "No supper tonight."

"Actually," Harper said. "Abel found some dehydrated rations in his cabin. They are enough to last a week or so if we're very careful."

Relieved, Rance nodded at Harper. "I'm glad Abel is willing to share his secret stash with us."

"I think he forgot about them."

Sure he did. But Rance was grateful, even though the discovery of the rations only made her feel a tad better. She sank down on the bench at the table and stared ahead, looking down the short, darkened hallway that led to the crew's quarters on the bottom level. Harper, Abel, and Tally each had a tiny cabin down that corridor.

Maybe Tally should have been Captain, Rance thought in disgust. He'd certainly do a better job than she was doing at the moment.

Solaris walked into the galley wearing his flight suit. He'd changed his face into the one the crew was used to seeing— easy, boyish good looks and a mop of brown hair. That wasn't his true appearance, either. Rance had never seen the real one. Right now, that irritated her too.

He sat down across from her and stewed, ready to continue the argument if Rance gave him a reason. Harper sensed the tension between them and busied herself with making her favorite herbal tea. After setting a cup in front of each of them, she sat next to Rance and looked at Solaris.

He stared morosely into his cup as if he wished it were something stronger.

"You can't help that we didn't get any food, Solaris," Harper said.

Solaris glanced up, his eyes sharp with criticism. "No, that's the Captain's fault."

Rance rolled her eyes.

Harper frowned and said, "The captain's not to blame for our current predicament."

She glared pointedly at him, and Solaris had the grace to look sheepishly back to his tea. Harper was referring to Solaris' status as a fugitive, the most wanted man in the galaxy. They had risked their necks to hide him.

Feeling vindicated, and particularly grateful to Harper, Rance sipped her tea. It was smooth and fruity and savory all at the same time. Good thing it tasted good because it was supper. They'd make those rations last as long as possible.

Harper had never contradicted Solaris before. If gentle Harper was snapping, Rance *knew* it was time to move on. They could find another short run in this system, to tie them over until they landed a bigger job. She was about to say something when James' voice came over the ship's comm.

"Hey, Captain, hate to interrupt the family meeting, but we have a message from Prometheus."

"Prometheus? Who do I know on Prometheus?"

Rance's mind whirled with questions and possibilities as she abandoned her mug on the table and sprinted out of the galley.

She took the stairs two at a time. Down the straight corridor, past her own quarters, then two more tiny cabins—Solaris' and James'. Then up the ladder into the cramped cockpit.

It overflowed with buttons and screens. Rance's long legs felt crammed in every time she sat in her seat behind the pilot's, which was pushed up close to the large window.

The windows were Rance's favorite part of the ship. One above, one in front. Despite the fact the area was small, Rance loved coming up to stargaze when they weren't in hyperspace. She'd put up with any situation, as long as she got to return to see the stars after a long day of work.

Today, James had darkened the windows to keep out the glare of the afternoon sun. But they weren't so dark Rance couldn't see the yellow sky and look out over the vast expanse of green and purple fields all the way to the river.

"No supper then, huh?" he asked, running a hand through his shaggy red hair.

"Who is it?" Rance asked as she sat in her chair. She sank into the plush seat and propped her feet onto the console in front of her.

"Someone named Moira Finn," James said, eyeing her dirty boots.

"Moira!"

"Know her?"

"We grew up together on Xanthes. She did the *proper* thing and got married as soon as she turned eighteen. Wonder how she found me."

"Maybe through one of our usual contacts? She sent you a video."

Rance frowned. Moira didn't associate with the sort of crowd the *Star Streaker* deemed *contacts*. If she'd gone to all that trouble, something wasn't right. An anxious knot formed in Rance's stomach. If Moira could track her down enough to send a message, Davos could too.

It was undoubtedly time to leave.

Rance glanced out the window, expecting Unity ships to descend on them right then. But the sky was still clear and yellow, so she said, "Play the message, Deliverance."

Yes, Captain. Playing message from Lady Moira Finn.

Rance had hoped to find a way to get Deliverance to speak audibly. For some reason, it hadn't been programmed into her code. Harper had been working round the clock to fix it, but even she couldn't find a way inside to work on it. They'd asked Deliverance herself how to do it, but the AI adamantly refused to help them.

Of course, Rance *would* inherit an AI that was stubborn.

For now, Deliverance's words overlaid Moira Finn's face as it popped up against the backdrop of a sheer, purple curtain made of expensive fabric. Moira had dark, curly hair arranged artfully around high cheekbones and a smooth brow. She had always been classically beautiful, and a life of wealth and ease hadn't hurt her at all.

Today, though, her beautiful face contrasted sharply with the fear in her eyes. Concerned, Rance leaned forward in her seat and braced herself for bad news about her family. It was the only logical purpose for Moira's message.

James glanced at the captain's expression and then moved around to watch over her shoulder. Rance didn't object. She didn't have any secrets from James, and Moira couldn't possibly tell her anything she wouldn't share with her crew.

"Devri," Moira began, using Rance's real name. "I hope this gets to you in time. I've gone over and over my options, but I don't have any, really. I heard you had your own ship—money is no object."

Moira paused and looked up at something behind the camera. Then she lowered her voice. "My husband is missing."

She spoke so low Rance had to turn up the volume to hear.

"He's been gone eight days. And during that time, strange events have taken place. Things aren't right on Prometheus. I can't explain everything, but I need to get off this planet. I don't know who to trust. A few families have already left, but I'm afraid to ask others to take me with them. No one seems to have heard from Richard or wants to talk about him. I can't explain, but I think he's in trouble, if not d-dead."

Moira's voice broke. She looked behind the camera again with a wild look in her eyes. Then she leaned close to it, her fine nose pressing against the lens.

She whispered, almost inaudibly, "Come get me."

Then the video went black.

"Come get her?" James asked. "Is that for real?"

Rance pushed the screen away from her and sat back. "Moira always was a bit dramatic. But this is weird."

"I'll say. Is Davos behind it?"

Rance looked up at James. "You think it's a trap?"

James shrugged. "Don't know what to think, but yeah, could be. How well do you know Moira?"

"Not very well. Our parents moved in the same circles. I saw her at society balls, that kind of thing. If Davos was trying to lure me to Prometheus, he could have picked a closer friend from my childhood."

James opened his mouth in mock surprise. "You mean you had *friends* as a child? You were allowed to have them, being the precious heir to the House of Davos? I'm surprised you weren't kept in a soft, pillowy room at the top of a windowless tower."

"Very funny. Yes, I had *friends*. But I parted ways with many of them when I went to the Flight Academy."

"Moira was one of them?"

"Yes. She wasn't a bad sort, just a typical, pampered princess."

"Like you."

Rance grinned and looked at her friend. "I was pampered, James, but never typical."

"So what are we going to do?"

She tapped her fingers against her armrest. "We know we have to leave Ares, anyway. Moira will pay us—she's good for it. And we just lost our last fifty in the market."

"Lost?"

"Long story. Ask Solaris. Speaking of—"

Rance pressed a button and called the CO up to the cockpit. As always, when he emerged into the tiny space, Rance was reminded of just how small the cockpit was—Solaris was a good two inches taller than she. He barely fit.

"Alright, CO," she said. "What do you think about a trip to Prometheus?"

"You mean as a pleasure trip? A family vacation?"

"Ha, ha. I meant on a mission."

Solaris smiled, his first actual smile in a week. "You mean a mission where we'll get paid?"

The grin was infectious. Rance smiled back. "Yeah. A friend of mine wants to pay us to get her off Prometheus."

"What's wrong on Prometheus?"

James pulled up Moira's video and played it for Solaris. When it was done, Solaris frowned. "Do you know her well?"

"I agree it's weird, but we can't just ignore her."

"It worries me that something is happening on Prometheus that we don't know about."

"James," Rance said, "Let's check reports from Prometheus."

James spent a few moments in his chair, checking for any unusual activity from the Core planet. When he didn't find anything, he turned around and shook his head.

Rance looked back at Solaris. "If we need to disguise the ship, can you still do that?"

Solaris had been exhausted after the last time he'd had to disguise the *Star Streaker*.

"I can. Let's be careful, huh?"

"Always," Rance said.

"What is *that*?" Rance asked.

She stood at the top of the stair, looking down into the cargo bay. They were about to leave. Rance was going over her last checklist before takeoff. Harper, James, and Tally were looking at something in Abel's arms—something furry and squeaking.

They parted, and Abel turned toward the captain, sporting a black eye. A small, furry bundle of ginger fluff sat in his large hands. Strange, high-pitched noises emanated from it.

It was a cappatter.

"*No,*" she said.

"Aww, boss, they were going to throw it into the river for the lantess."

James snickered. "Looks like they tried to throw *you* into the river too."

"Yeah, well," Abel said, looking sheepish. "I had to fight them over it. Then they threw the little guy at me and walked off laughing."

Rance stomped down the stairs, letting her heavy magnetic boots clang on the metal a little louder than necessary. "We are *not* bringing one of those onboard. They get into everything."

The little creature squirmed in Abel's hands. It looked like a fuzzy ball. When she reached Abel, the cappatter opened sad, blue eyes and looked accusingly at Rance.

Then, three little hairless arms shot out from where they'd been hiding in its fur. They reached for Rance, and the cappatter wiggled three little fingers on each tiny hand.

"See, boss? It likes you."

Rance crossed her arms and glared determinedly at Abel. "No pets."

"It's not one of the rules, Captain," Harper said.

Rance scoffed. "It's a given rule of space travel! Pets on a spaceship are a nuisance. They get underfoot. They wreak havoc with the cleaning systems. And they distract crews from their work."

"Nobles travel with them all the time," Abel said. "I saw them on Triton."

Rance's nostrils flared. "How many of them were smugglers—"

"Anonymous transporters," James added helpfully.

"*Anonymous transporters*," she said through gritted teeth.

"We won't let it be a nuisance, boss," Abel said. "Promise."

The cappatter squeaked again, and three more arms appeared. Then, it hopped out of Abel's hands onto Rance's shoulder like some sort of round, hairy spider.

The critter was light, its fur soft and silky. It nuzzled Rance's ear, tickling her earlobe. She refused to look at it.

"We'll keep it with us," Harper said. "You won't even know it's here."

The cappatter rubbed a smooth, hairless hand over Rance's cheek, petting her. She swatted its hand away. "No. Cappatters are pets for children."

Tally sniffed. "Well then, it'll be right at home," he said, looking pointedly at James.

Abel's eyes glazed over with a dreamy, nostalgic look. "I had one as a kid. It was blue, not ginger. Used to sleep with me every night—until my older brother stole it and gave it to his girlfriend. My dad wouldn't buy me another one. He said I was too old for another pet."

The cappatter wrapped four of its six arms around Rance's head as far as they would go. They squeezed her while one little hand grabbed her nose. Its hand was hot and smelled like warm cinnamon.

"No," she said again, this time with a little less enthusiasm.

"Didn't you ever have a pet, boss?"

Rance gripped the creature with both hands, trying to pry it off her face. "My father didn't allow them. He said pets made nobles weak."

"But you're not a noblewoman anymore," Harper said. "*And*, you aren't like your father."

Rance sighed. "That's a dirty trick, Harper. You know I'm not like him."

Harper grinned and shot James a look that said, *got her*.

Rance finally managed to tug the creature off her shoulder and held it up to look at. It wriggled, trying to get back to her face.

"Hold still, fur ball."

It obeyed, training its soft eyes on her again, holding her attention. With its blue eyes and ginger hair, it almost looked like—

Rance burst out laughing, and the cappatter squeaked happily.

"It looks like Solaris!" she said. She laughed harder, bringing the CO out of engineering.

Solaris walked over to the group, grinning, anticipating a good joke. "What looks like—*no*."

Then, he sneezed violently.

The cappatter squealed in fright.

James grabbed it from Rance and held it close. "You scared it, Solaris! Don't do that!"

Solaris sniffed and said, "I'm allergic to those things."

"I guess that settles it then," Rance said, with the tiniest twinge of regret. She squashed it down. "We can't keep it."

"Oh no, Captain," Harper said. "I'm sure I can come up with something to alleviate his allergies. That's not a problem."

Solaris turned his own pleading eyes on Rance. "Please no," he said.

But now that Rance had made the connection between the cappatter and Solaris, she couldn't get the resemblance out of her mind.

"Harper says she can help. And the thugs were going to throw it in the river."

Harper, Abel, and James let out whoops of joy. The cappatter squeaked happily again. Tally scowled at all of them with his large, green eyes, like the crew members were out of their minds.

"Keep it out of the engine room," he ordered Abel. "I don't want to find hair everywhere."

Then he turned and stalked over to the fold-out crash chairs in the hold. Everything was ready for the *Streaker* to leave.

"What are you going to name it, Abel?" James asked as the cappatter nuzzled his hands.

"Henry."

Solaris snorted.

Abel glared at him and took Henry away from James.

"It's the name I had for the one when I was a kid. *Hey, little Henry.*"

Henry blinked at Abel and then wound its arms through his fingers.

The sight of Abel's wide, powerful, tattooed frame cradling the fluffy ginger ball was more than Rance could handle. She stifled a snicker. Then she accidentally caught Solaris' eye, and they both had to hurry upstairs to the cockpit before they burst out laughing.

"I didn't have the heart to tease him about it," Rance said when she'd calmed down.

James followed them to the cockpit, and they all strapped into their seats.

Before they could complete take-off procedures, Henry found them. He climbed the ladder, scuttled across the floor, and wrapped himself around Solaris' leg.

Solaris sneezed again. And vainly tried to shake the cappatter off.

"Abel!" Rance called.

Abel appeared to pry Henry off Solaris' leg. "Sorry, boss!"

"He's cute," James said, "but keep him out of the cockpit."

"Hear, hear," Solaris added. Then he sneezed again.

Although Abel whisked the creature away, the damage had already been done, and they had to delay take off until Solaris' sneezing fit subsided.

"Wonder why they were going to throw Henry into the river?" James asked as he guided the *Star Streaker* out of the spaceport.

"Can't imagine why," Solaris said, blowing his nose

loudly. Tears streamed down his cheeks from his red, irritated eyes.

Rance watched the bright river shrink to a sparkling thread amongst the patchwork of fields. "Abel didn't say. They're expensive little things to throw away."

"Well, he's ours now."

Solaris moaned and muttered something like "perfect" under his breath.

CHAPTER TWO

No ONE on the *Star Streaker* was sorry to leave Ares. After two months with nothing to do and little food, the crew came alive with a new burst of energy. So much energy that the five-day hyperspace trip to Prometheus felt like a vacation.

They used the time well. Without supplies to inventory, they made a plan of action for when they landed and assigned roles to everyone. Since no one knew the situation on Prometheus, all felt a little apprehensive. And yet Rance couldn't help feeling excited about their destination. Even if Davos was waiting for her at the end of their journey, she was confident they could escape.

The only person who frequently expressed doubts was Tally. His main concern was being recognized on Prometheus. Rance had been there many times as a teenager. Her family owned a house there. Tally had made frequent trips himself, always as Davos' servant. For years, Tally had gone everywhere Davos went. And he would be recognized anywhere Davos would be recognized.

In this case, Rance had the advantage over Tally. She didn't look like the same person who had accompanied her father on trips to Prometheus, Barton, and Triton. Her features hadn't changed much except to mature a bit, but without the luxurious clothing, exotic headdresses, and diamond-crusted makeup of Xanthes, she would have little trouble walking around the streets without being recognized. Tally, however, had no such disguises to his appearance.

So, Rance created a workaround. James, Harper, and Tally would remain on the *Star Streaker* with the "engines running" while Rance, Solaris, and Abel went to find Moira. Rance hoped once they landed, she would be able to contact her old friend and get her exact location. She knew Moira's home was close to Davos' in the towering residences of the politicians and noblemen. A quick call to Moira and they'd be on their way. Once they found her, they'd get to the *Star Streaker* and take off before anyone noticed they were there.

"Do you want to relay a message to her now?" James asked later that first day.

"No," Rance said. "We don't know who could be listening. And if it's intercepted by the wrong people, we don't know what dragon's dung will be waiting for us when we arrive."

That night when she lay in bed, Rance considered all the possible things that could go wrong on Prometheus. What if they were recognized? What if they couldn't find Moira? What if she'd already left?

What if, what if, what if?

Just when Rance had finally dozed off, something fluffy nuzzled her hand. Startled, she sat up and shook the blanket before she realized it was Henry. He flew across the room, squealing in surprise. Or was it delight? All his squeals sounded the same. A soft, muffled thud against the wall, another on the floor. Then, silence.

Had she accidentally killed it? Rance turned on the light just in time to see a long arm disappear into one of her magnetic boots.

"Hey, you. Get out of there. How'd you get in here, anyway?"

A ginger tuft of hair appeared at the top of her boot, and Henry's blue eyes peered back at her.

"I mean it—*out*."

When Henry didn't move, Rance got out of bed and grabbed him. He resisted, holding onto the inside of her boot until she shook him. He let go of the heavy boot, and it fell right onto Rance's big toe. Shooting pain ran through her toe and into her foot.

"Son of an asteroid worm!" she yelled, dropping Henry to grab her foot.

The cappatter fell to the floor, unharmed, while Rance nursed her sore toe. Within seconds, it swelled to three times its normal size, and she couldn't move it without gritting her teeth in pain. Her eyes watered.

Henry whimpered and stretched out its arms to be held.

"Get. Out."

A knock, and then, "Captain?"

James.

"Come in," she called.

The door opened, and James peered in. His normally tidy hair looked bristly and stuck up on one side.

"You have the worst bedhead I've ever seen," Rance said. She wasn't feeling too humorous at the moment, but teasing James was better than thinking about the pain in her foot.

James swept his eyes over Henry, Rance holding her foot, and the magnetic boot on the floor.

"You swore so loudly I think they heard you on Triton."

"Get this menace out of here."

"Aw, Rance—"

Rance glared at him, cutting him off. "I think I broke my toe. It's Henry's fault."

"How'd he get in here?"

"How should I know? All I know is I was accosted in my sleep."

Henry's eyes changed from soft blue to bright and watery.

"You've made him cry, Captain!"

"I've made *him* cry? Get him out and help me get down to the med bay."

"Yes, Captain."

James picked up the doleful creature and cradled it like he would cradle a child. The action was slightly discon- certing for Rance, who always thought of James as an adult- sized child.

He walked out, his bare feet ringing softly on the metal floor all the way down the corridor.

Then, Solaris appeared, looking only slightly less disheveled than James.

"What's up?"

"Glad to know you're quick on your feet when there's trouble," she said with as much sarcasm as she could muster. "I was attacked."

Solaris sneezed before saying, "What?"

"Henry."

"Henry attacked you?"

"No, my boot. Help me up."

He walked over and put an arm under her shoulder. Rance stood, gingerly placing her right foot down on the floor, testing her weight.

"I'm confused," Solaris said. "Why does your room smell like cinnamon cappatter?"

Then, he sneezed again. Since he was holding onto Rance, she shook with him. He gripped her tighter, which wasn't too helpful since it forced her to put her weight forward onto her sore toe.

More tears sprang to her eyes.

"You know," she said when he had recovered, "I've had worse injuries than this, but there's something more annoying about a broken toe than any other broken bone."

"I can think of more annoying things. Would you like me to list them, Captain?" With the prospect of having a paying job, some of Solaris' easy humor had returned.

"No. I'm in too much pain."

"Are you going to whine all night?"

"It's my toe. I'll whine if I want to."

Solaris looked at her, his eyes meeting hers a moment longer than necessary.

"I think we're breaking a rule," he said.

"It's not a rule if someone needs help."

"Does that apply to the other rules too?" Solaris asked mischievously. "For instance, if I see you need help, and a swear word accidentally slips out because, you know, you're in danger, would that be okay?"

"Let's not test it."

"You never actually told me what the consequences were for breaking the rules, Captain."

Rance was tall, and her room had never been very big. With Solaris' height, he seemed to take up the rest of the space. Suddenly, with his proximity, and the tiny room, her quarters felt small indeed.

Feeling a bit disconcerted, she pulled away. "I guess if you're going to stand here joking instead of helping me get to the med bay, I'll hop down there by myself."

Solaris let go and then sneezed again. "It's a fair question."

"We're not breaking a rule, Solaris. You're not my *companion*."

"Oh?"

"The rule says *no companions in quarters*."

"That could be interpreted in a number of ways. But ah well."

Rance pushed past him and hobbled out into the hall.

James was climbing the stairs, looking disappointed. "I gave Henry back to Abel."

"Abel needs to make a box or cage to keep him in. That fur ball is going to mess something up if he's left to roam the ship on his own."

Sensing Rance's stormy mood, James had the good sense to stay quiet. His eyes flicked to Solaris, who was now standing in the corridor behind Rance. After exchanging glances, the two men moved to help her at the same time in a flurry of false chivalry.

She waved them off. "I've got it. Just make sure I don't fall down the stairs and break my neck, too. Something tells me that would be worse than a broken toe."

"You said nothing was worse than a broken toe," Solaris said. She couldn't see him, but she almost *heard* the wink directed at her.

"I said—oh never mind."

Solaris smirked. Despite Rance shooting annoyed looks at them all the way, James and Solaris insisted on accompanying her to the med bay. Once there, Rance stared at the small, enclosed emergency hospital pod with dread. She hated tight spaces. The cramped ship was fine, but something about laying down inside the chamber and having it close over her sent a nasty shiver down her spine.

"I wonder if I can just stick my foot in without having to lock my whole body into it," she said after a moment.

"It might mistake your foot for a foreign body," James said, "instead of the human appendage that it is. With that bruising and swelling, I wouldn't blame it."

"It's smarter than that," Rance said. "Deliverance, how do I fix a broken toe without getting into the emergency surgery pod?"

Text shot across Rance's ZOD, her optic lens.

Get Harper.

"Oh. Great. The smartest AI in the empire has learned sarcasm."

"I wonder where she got it from?" Solaris said with another smirk, reading Deliverance's answer on the screen.

"It's not sarcasm, Cap," James said. "She's telling us to get Harper."

"What?"

Forgetting the pain it would cause in her toe, Rance spun around to look at the screen. Another line of code was sitting on it, one that hadn't shown up on her ZOD. "What does it say?"

"It's jumbled up. Harper will know." James strode out of the med bay, presumably to get Harper.

Rance hobbled over to look at the screen, wincing as each step caused pain to shoot up her foot. The top of her toe had turned a nice, nasty shade of black. Along with the swelling, James had been correct—it didn't look much like a toe at all.

Solaris studied the code a minute. "Harper won't know, either. It's a bunch of gobbledygook—doesn't make sense."

"Is that the official diagnosis? Gobbledygook?"

"Best way to describe it."

"So now you know code from a Tritonian sync?"

"I know a lot of things."

"Hmph."

Solaris turned to her. "Just because I don't tell *you*."

"Why didn't you tell me you know about Deliverance?"

"I don't know about Deliverance. But I know code. And this is nonsense."

"Let's just wait for Harper, shall we?" Rance said irritably.

When Harper entered the med bay, her hair spiky as always, she tried to examine Rance's foot.

"Look at the code first," Rance said.

Harper studied it a minute, her frown deepening. She moved her head from side to side, reading it from different angles, and then shook her head. "Looks like gobbledygook to me."

Solaris shot Rance a smug look.

"Well, let's figure it out," Rance said. "I don't want any hiccups on this tr—"

The ship made an odd humming noise, changing pitch from a gentle resonance to a harsh vibrato. The floor shook, and Rance gripped the table next to her for support, anticipating something worse.

When nothing else happened, they breathed a sigh of relief.

"What in Triton's fuzzy beard was that?" James asked.

And then the lights went out, clicking off all at once like someone had flipped a master switch. Screens blipped and went dark. Button lights faded black. The darkness in the med bay was complete.

No one moved.

"That wasn't a hiccup," James said. "That was a belch."

"We're not weightless," Harper remarked, a disembodied voice in the dark. "Gravity control is still working."

"What about atmosphere?" Rance asked. "Are life support systems still working?"

"We'll have to go to engineering to check," Solaris said. "James, go get Tally."

"Yeah, sure, no problem. Just need to find—" James groped his way through the med bay and stumbled over Rance's broken toe.

"OW!" More tears streamed down her face. At least no one could see them.

"Sorry, Captain, looking for the door."

"Oh for the Founders' sake!" Harper said, borrowing one of Rance's phrases. They heard her rummage around. And then a light flashed on. She handed it to Solaris, who pointed it at the drawer Harper had been in.

"I keep these glow-lights stored all over the ship," Harper said. "Although I never thought you all would lose your heads if we went dark. The battery will last forever. Longer than any of us if the carbon dioxide levels shoot up."

They passed lights around. Rance felt foolish about her lapse of common sense. She blamed it on the toe.

"We've got to check everything," she said. "Ventilation, hydration, coolant, engines, refrigeration, hyperdrive."

James left to get Tally and Abel, muttering about how they could sleep through anything. Harper climbed into the control room in the nose of the ship.

"The hyperdrive's still working, Captain," Solaris said. "We haven't stopped."

As if on cue, the humming changed again. This time the ship vibrated until Rance's teeth rattled. When it stopped, they were in complete silence.

"Well," she said. She had decided to counter her recent foray into panic with practicality. "Glad to know not much else can go wrong. Power, hyperdrive—"

"Don't say anything else," Solaris warned. "You'll jinx us. There's a whole host of other problems we can't deal with right now. If the life support systems go, we're done."

Despite the situation, Rance laughed. "I don't believe in jinxes. There's something wrong with the ship, nothing that can't be explained. And the life support systems are separate from the main power. Solaris, you act like you've never been on a spaceship before."

"No need to be condescending. I didn't know."

Rance pulled a mock face. "You mean no one told you? We knew something you didn't? How terrible for you. Deliverance!" she said hotly. "What's the status of the life support systems?"

No answer.

"She's not responding, Captain," Harper called from the control room. "Not to voice commands or commands from my handset."

Rance peeked her head up into the tiny control room. Harper sat in the middle of a room jammed with screens, buttons, and levers.

"The network is down too, then," Rance said. "I can't access anything through my implant."

James returned with Tally and Abel. Abel wasn't wearing a shirt, revealing his bulging muscles and blue, body-covering tattoos that depicted everything from an old girl-friend to a Triton security stamp to a rampaging, fire-breathing dragon.

He carried Henry in his arms.

"What's the dragon for?" Rance asked, trying not to laugh at him holding the furry creature.

Abel shrugged. "When I was a kid, I always wanted to see one. Then I found out they were myths. It was worse than finding out there isn't a Santa Kringle."

"What's Santa Kringle?" James asked.

Abel gaped at him. "You don't know?" He looked at Rance as if expecting her to confirm something.

She shrugged and said, "James grew up poor in the Outer Colonies. They don't know about Santa Kringle there. Santa Kringle takes gifts to children."

James looked offended. "He didn't bring me gifts."

Solaris cleared his throat. The three turned to him.

"Right," Rance said, returning to the present. "Solaris, stay here and help Harper. James, go with Tally and see if he needs help. Abel, I want a thorough check of every physical space on this ship you can get into. Make a list of everywhere you can't squeeze, and James or Harper will follow up with those in a bit."

"Yes, Captain," they all said.

Rance headed up to the cockpit, limping along like a giant sea turtle swimming through molasses. The swelling had spread to her foot, but she didn't have time to fix it now. They were drifting out in empty space and still didn't know where.

In the cockpit, faraway stars shone through the windows like tiny pinpricks of light. Rance sank into the pilot's chair and turned off her light. The room became immediately dark, with no starlight close enough to illuminate their situation.

That wasn't a bad thing. If they'd sputtered out of hyperspace close to a star system, it could mean they were in hostile territory. Pirates were notorious for staking claims to barren rocks orbiting lone stars.

Rance had no way of checking their location. They were blind. She flipped a few switches, desperately wishing one of them would jump-start everything. But she knew better than to waste much time. Nothing would be fixed from up here until they got power back to the consoles.

She pulled out her handset. "Anything yet, Harper?"

"Not yet, Captain."

"Where are we?" James asked.

"Nowhere specific. Somewhere in the DEEP."

The DEEP stood for Deep Exploration Extraction Point. Originally, colonization crews and explorers used it as a stopping point on their way to distant star systems. Because it lay in neutral territory, with no government claiming it, human or otherwise, the expanse of emptiness was perfect for scientists who wanted to study the stars in peace. However, due to increased pirate activity in recent years, the stations had been emptied, and colonization bases relocated.

Now, Rance liked to say DEEP stood for Deplorably Empty for the Expansion of Pirates.

"Find anything?" she asked nervously. She didn't like to think of pirates just now when the *Streaker* was stranded without the possibility of help if they needed it.

"The emergency lights in engineering work. So, there's that. Tally's still running checks. Life support is going strong."

Rance sighed in relief as she limped back to the ladder, sliding down it and landing on her good foot. On her way back downstairs, she stopped and grabbed her helmet from her room. The comm there would work. She put it on and lifted the visor. At least she wouldn't have to carry it in her hand now.

In the engine room, James held a bright light while Tally dove between the hyperdrive core and secondary engines. As always, engineering was spotless. Barely a speck of grease was on the floor. The room smelled of it though.

Tally sat amongst the disassembled pieces of the hyper-drive coils' casing, another tiny light between his teeth, shining onto intricate wiring. His eyes glowed green, but his dark body blended into his surroundings, leaving the strange illusion of disembodied eyes floating in the dark.

"Find anything?" Rance asked.

"So far, nothing," he mumbled with the light. "I thought something here might have shorted during the outage and caused a chain reaction. But everything here looks in perfect order." He moved away. "See where that line of wires connects to the main power feed?"

Rance looked, but most of it looked the same to her. Then, she saw where he pointed—a tiny bundle of wires snaking their way toward the casing.

"Yes."

"If the drive had shorted out, you would see scorch marks on these wires, possibly even some broken ones. But they are intact. No burning smell, either. Of course, the *Streaker* has fail-safes to make sure that doesn't happen, but I've seen it on other ships before. It's not entirely unheard of, if the power surge is catastrophic enough."

"Where'd you learn all this, Tally?" James asked.

Tally looked affronted. "You've known me for five years, James, and you're just now asking?"

"I've wondered before, but you don't like questions."

"There's a reason for that," Tally snapped.

"Well, excuse me for caring."

"You don't care, James. You are simply curious. I am old enough to know the difference."

Annoyed, Rance rolled her eyes. The two of them always found something to argue about. In truth, she didn't know much about Tally's past beyond the years he'd worked for her father. She didn't even know how old he was. Graekens lived longer than humans, and she'd often wondered if he weren't hundreds of years old.

The comm turned on with a click.

"Captain," Harper said. "We found something."

"There's nothing wrong with the ship," Harper said. "There's something wrong with Deliverance."

"How do you know?" Rance asked. She squeezed in beside Solaris, who was holding onto the ladder and looking up into the control room.

"The Caducean Drive she's installed on is silent. I should be able to link to it from my handset even without main power, but the drive is dead."

"Couldn't it have been from the power surge?"

"I don't think so. This is an expensive, extravagant piece of equipment, even if it doesn't look like that from the outside. It has its own surge protectors built in. It won't go dark from a simple power hiccup. I think it went dark and *caused* the hiccup. And something is preventing me from restarting all the systems."

"You think Deliverance is stopping you."

"Yes, and I can't figure out why."

"Maybe there's some danger we don't know about?"

Solaris shook his head. "It's dangerous for us to drift about like this in deep space. We could starve to death, or freeze, or get picked up by pirates. Deliverance must think that rebooting the main power is more dangerous than any of those things."

Rance shuddered. "None of those are good options. All of them are certain death. If we need to take a chance, I'd rather take it trying to fix the ship. Any chance of Deliverance fixing it herself?"

"Not if the drive is malfunctioning."

"Then unplug it."

Harper raised her eyebrows. "Captain? We're not sure what will happen."

A sinking feeling settled into Rance's stomach. Apparently having an AI onboard the *Streaker* was not in her stars after all. She fumed at the amount of trouble it had caused. "We know what will happen if we don't do anything. Pull it."

Harper grabbed the drive, took one last look at Rance, and then pulled. It slid out of its slot with ease. Rance breathed a sigh of relief. She had half-expected it to be stuck in there.

They waited, expecting something bad to happen, anything, really.

"How long will it take to reboot, Harper?"

"A couple of hours. I'll bring everything back online one system at a time, to check for anomalies."

"Can we get lights first? I need to fix my toe."

"Lights aren't a problem."

Harper pressed a few buttons, and a flashing cursor came up on the screen in front of her. It was reassuring to know they would be up and running soon. After a few more lines of command, lights came on throughout the ship.

Rance switched off her glow-light. "I want to check and double-check every system before we jump into hyperspace. Take as much time as you need, Harper."

"Yes, Captain."

The order was unnecessary. Harper wouldn't let anything slip by her. She'd triple check everything, and then check it again, before allowing any attempt to restart the engines.

Solaris followed Rance back into the med bay. Since Harper was busy, she found a medical manual on her handset and looked up how to set her toe without putting it in the emergency pod. Then, she hopped up onto the other table.

"I think Harper has some injectable stuff stored in one of

these refrigerators, to help with the swelling," Rance said. "Get it, will you?"

Solaris obeyed, pulling supplies from the storage unit and spreading them out on the table next to Rance. An x-ray scanner revealed her toe was fractured in two places. He injected a local anesthetic into it, bringing her immediate relief. Rance held the portable scanner over it while Solaris set the bone back into place.

Then, more injections for swelling and infection.

"We have a healing compound in there," Harper called down. "Inject her bone with that. It will burn like heck but the fractures will heal within a few hours."

"How long will it take if I don't?" Rance asked.

"Two weeks, maybe three before you'd notice a difference, and you'd have stay off of it."

"That's not going to work. I need to walk around. We'll be on Prometheus in a few days."

Rance hated the idea of using valuable medical supplies, but she needed the use of her feet. There wasn't an option.

Solaris found the injectable, carefully packaged in a bubble-like bag. When he inserted the needle into her bone, it burned like he'd injected liquid fire into her body. Rance gritted her teeth and closed her eyes.

"On Triton," he said, "they have nanobots that will repair broken bones."

"And that emergency pod over there is calibrated to use them if necessary. But we don't keep them stocked. They are ridiculously expensive."

"All done," Solaris said, releasing her foot.

The pain had subsided. Rance hopped off the table, careful not to put weight on her foot.

"Where are you going?" Solaris asked.

"In case you hadn't noticed, we have work to do."

"We can't do much until Harper gets the power back on. Why don't you rest and reset yourself?"

"Why do you think I need *resetting*?"

Solaris sighed in frustration. "I didn't mean anything by it."

"Thanks, but I'll go up to the cockpit and wait."

He shrugged. "Yes, Captain."

Rance would have stormed out, but her numb toe prevented her from doing more than a hurried wobble out the door.

She didn't know why she'd become angry with him. Solaris was inherently helpful, a part of his character she rather liked. But Rance didn't like feeling helpless or showing real weakness in front of anybody.

Especially Solaris.

Why she felt that way, she couldn't say exactly. She'd always been competitive. Maybe it had something do with the fact that she always had the sense he could beat her at just about anything, even when he wasn't trying.

Rance climbed into the cockpit and sat in her customary chair. She leaned back, looking up at the stars that dotted the blackness around them. Gazing up at them reminded her of home on Xanthes. She always watched the stars as a child, falling asleep in the solarium as the wind and dust swirled around outside, blocking them out.

Soon, the lack of sleep and the pain medication took its toll, and she fell asleep without meaning to.

When James came up the ladder, Rance woke with a

start. The cockpit was lit up like twinkle lights, with all the usual glowing buttons and screens.

"Sleeping on the job, Captain?" he asked.

Rance's mouth was dry, the result of sleeping with her mouth wide open.

"What's up, James?"

"We have power to the engines and auxiliary systems. The consoles are functional. Just need to do some double-checking, but I think we're in the clear."

"That's it?" Rance refused to believe it was that simple.

"Harper tried to uninstall Deliverance, but the AI is bedded down on the hardware itself. However, since the Caducean Drive was removed, she seems to have deactivated."

"What does that mean for continuing our journey?"

James sat down in the pilot's chair and swiveled it around to look her. "Theoretically, we should be okay to jump into hyperspace."

"What about realistically?"

James smiled. "That too."

Rance smiled in relief. "Okay then. Don't tell anyone I was sleeping up here."

James smirked. "Wouldn't dream of it, Captain."

"I mean it."

"You're so paranoid, Cap."

"I detest drifting about in deep space, where anybody could come along and make easy prey of us. And stop calling me Cap. That's an order."

"As you wish."

"Argh! James!"

James laughed. "You must be tired if you let that get to

you. Go on, get some real sleep. I'll call you when we're ready."

"Nope. Not happening. Everyone else has been up, too. I'm not going to let a little injury get in the way of sharing the workload. Where's Henry?"

"Sleeping in Abel's spare boot."

"Hmph."

"Captain," Harper called over the comm. "It's taking less time than I thought to boot up. We should be ready to jump in ten minutes."

"Really?"

"Yes, Captain."

Solaris chimed in over the comm. "Maybe you should go to sleep on the job more often, Captain. That way we can get some work done around here without you breathing over our shoulders. Although with that loud snoring—"

"I don't breathe over your shoulders! Wait—"

James snorted and then burst out laughing.

"You told them."

He held up his hand as if Rance had thrown something at him. She *was* contemplating it.

"You were snoring, Captain. I couldn't let a good thing like that go to waste!"

"What did you do?"

"Hologrammed the whole thing," Solaris said, the mirth in his voice unmistakable. "Sent it to all the screens and holos onboard, which were all working, by the way."

James snickered again and stood. "Your mouth was wide open too."

Rance reached over and punched his arm.

Just then, Solaris climbed into the cockpit and sat in his chair. The traces of his laughter were all over his face.

"Glad somebody's in a better mood," Rance grumbled.

"Why shouldn't I be? We're going to be back in hyperspace soon, heading to our original destination and possibly a good meal. I'm so hungry I could eat Henry. Although, I don't want to pick hair from my teeth. And I'm not crazy about cinnamon."

"Not funny," Abel called over the comm. Then, "He didn't mean it, Henry."

"Just kidding, Abel," Solaris said. "Just kidding."

"He is just kidding, Abel," Tally said over the comm. "Sit back down."

While Tally convinced Abel not to go to the cockpit and beat Solaris to a pulp, Rance sat back in her chair and told everyone to harness in, as a precaution. "Get ready for the countdown to hyperspace jump. Coordinates loaded, Harper?"

"Yes, Captain."

Solaris did his pre-flight checks and nodded to Rance.

"Alright, James. Whenever you're ready."

Rance always liked this part. No matter how many jumps to hyperspace, she never tired of seeing the blue wave wash over the ship, of feeling the slight electrifying current in the air, the tingle on her tongue. The anticipation was delicious. It meant freedom. Rance breathed easy. They'd only lost a few hours, after all.

She was disappointed about Deliverance though. They'd only had her a short time, and—

James pressed a button, flipped a switch, and grabbed the throttle. "Jumping to hyperspace in three, two, one."

The ship spun up, the hum of the smooth drive more like a subconscious thought than a sound. A blue wave appeared around the window, blurring the stars.

And then it disappeared.

One by one, all systems shut down, lights turned off, the drive spun down, dead. The cockpit was in complete darkness. Once again, they were at the mercy of the void.

"Well, that was anticlimactic," James said.

"By all the Founders of Xanthes," Rance said, fuming. "Can't we get anything right today?"

"Are you implying we did something wrong, Captain?" James said. "Because everything checked out. It's annoying that you blame us."

"We still have some power," Solaris said. "Look."

A light flashed near his elbow. It came from a button labeled "Initiate" and was used to power up the ship on short notice.

"Tally, what's the status below?"

"Checking now, Captain."

Forgetting about her sore toe and her bare feet, Rance stood and stepped out into the aisle. She winced, but the pain was much better. It didn't look so bruised, either, but the swelling wasn't much better. It felt like she was wearing a giant's toe. Even the toenail had turned black. Rance made a mental note to ask Harper about it later.

Before she could get down the ladder, Harper reported in. "It's just a short, Captain. We've overloaded one of the main breakers. Probably when Deliverance kept trying to turn on before she was deactivated."

"Please tell me it won't take an expensive part we don't have to fix it."

"Okay. I won't tell you."

Rance groaned.

"But I can rig something to get us moving again. We'll need to make some replacements once we get to Prometheus."

"Fine. I'll come down and help you. Where's the panel?"

"It's one of the main dashboards for the hyperdrive coil. Outside the ship."

"That seems like a hazardous place to put it," Solaris said. "It's a major security flaw in the ship's design."

Tally chimed in. "The *Star Streaker* is a luxury space cruiser, not a military vessel. We need every available bit of space inside. Security doesn't trump comfort."

Rance swelled with pride at how Tally defended the *Star Streaker*. Anyway, it was just as much his ship as hers. He'd been there when she bought it and had been with her ever since. If it weren't for Tally, Rance wouldn't have made it as far as she had.

"I guess that settles it," she said. "Abel, suit up. You and I are going on a space walk."

Abel whooped so loudly, he didn't need the comm for her to hear. His excited voice carried all the way up from the hold.

But Rance had forgotten that her toe was the size of a vagrappe. When she returned to her quarters, it wouldn't fit in her boot.

"Guess I'm going then, Captain," Solaris said, watching her attempt to put on her magnetic boot from the corridor.

Rance sighed. "Okay, suit up."

Within a few minutes, they were suited up and Abel was standing inside the tiny airlock. They all waited impatiently as the compartment slowly depressurized. The air hissed out like the ship had a leak, rather than intentional cycling out air. Since the airlock was so small, Solaris had to wait until Abel was outside the ship with the hatch locked. Then they would repeat the process.

"Tally," Rance called. "Remind me to install a proper airlock on this ship someday. One that more than one person can use at the same time and doesn't take ten minutes."

"Noted, Captain, along with automatic gravity controls, a military-grade weapons system, larger lavatories, and an automatic peanut sheller."

"You just added that last one."

"No, Captain. Added two months, five days, and three hours ago."

"That's not too much to ask for," Solaris called. His voice sounded muffled in his space suit. Then, Abel gave the okay, and Solaris entered the airlock.

Rance waited impatiently. Soon, they would be visible through the cockpit windows, as the panel they needed was directly under the nose of the ship.

The ship clanged on the outside as their magnetic boots let them walk up the outer hull from the door. Rance imagined the quick catch-and-release from the magnets, the click as they engaged and disengaged, and sighed. She loved spacewalks.

Abel came into view and waved to her from outside. She waved back. He pretended to shove Solaris out away from the ship.

"Hey, knock it off," Rance ordered.

"You know, Captain," Solaris said. "I suddenly regret threatening to eat Henry."

"If Abel chucks you out into space, I'm not coming after you."

"You heard the boss. Hand me that socket wrench."

They worked several minutes, with a few clangs echoing inside the ship. For the most part, Rance let them work. Harper directed them from the body camera Solaris wore. Rance watched the work on her handset since the screens in the cockpit didn't have power.

After thirty minutes of tedious work, they had replaced the wiring and were reattaching the panel.

Then, a clang, and a strangled noise. It was muffled and came out with some indistinct but sharp syllables.

"Abel, you didn't disconnect Solaris' oxygen, did you?"

"No, Captain." Abel's voice was tight, controlled, like he was holding something in.

Rance couldn't tell if he was stifling laughter or fear. She must be tired if they both sounded the same. "Abel? Report."

"Solaris broke a rule," Abel said.

"Which one?"

"Well, not the ones about companions in quarters or drinking. It was in a different language. But *I* know what he said."

"Solaris? What's going on?"

"Uh, sorry, Captain," Solaris said finally, "but we have a problem."

"What is it?"

"We've got company."

CHAPTER THREE

"What is it?" Rance repeated.

"Well, I'm not an expert or anything, but it's metal and flying toward us. Looks like a ship."

"Harper!" Rance called, ignoring Solaris' sarcasm.

"Almost got it, Captain. Startup sequence running now. It won't take as long as last time because we didn't have a full shut down."

"Solaris, Abel, get inside."

"Already on our way."

Without lights or navigation or sensors, Rance was blind except for what she could see out the windows. She craned her neck, looking out from every angle possible. Then, she stepped on the chair and pushed her nose up to the glass.

Still nothing. The ship must have been approaching from behind.

"What kind of ship is it?" she asked. "Is it heading for us on purpose? What's its signature?"

Solaris' voice through Rance's handset sounded tinny.

"To answer your questions—can't tell, but it's big, yes, and I don't know."

There were three possibilities. It could have been a merchant ship, checking to see why the *Star Streaker* was drifting in deep space. It could have been a military ship—a Unity patrol. Or pirates.

Out of all the possibilities, pirates were the most logical. This far from nothing, the DEEP was a prime raiding location for pirate clans big and small. Unity patrols rarely patrolled anything but direct trade routes, and merchant ships and cruisers, afraid of a trap, wouldn't risk stopping for a foundering ship.

They needed to prepare. Rance waited anxiously for word that Abel and Solaris were inside. She didn't dare leave the cockpit, but she peeked down the ladder, listening for sounds of the airlock opening and closing. Not being able to see the ship approaching sent spikes of fear through her. Whoever they were, they hadn't hailed them, but they'd had plenty of time.

"Harper, ready?" Rance asked impatiently.

"Push the button, Captain."

"Solaris?"

"We're inside, Captain." From the sound of it, they had stripped out of their suits and were pounding up the stairs.

Rance hopped down off the chair, the pain in her toe registering only a little. She pushed the initiate button. The lights turned on in the cockpit, then down the corridor below. Instrument panels lit up, the comm dashboard to Rance's left switched on, and a moment later she was bringing up the radar screens that showed the unknown ship rapidly approaching.

Solaris and James appeared a moment later, taking their seats and running scans.

"How long until we can jump?" Rance asked the room.

"Five minutes. Still booting up."

"Tally? What's it looking like down there?"

"Perfect, although I'd be careful not to put too much stress on that hyperdrive coil, just as a precaution. We're all strapped in down here, Captain."

"James, I want a jump to hyperspace as soon as the drive registers ready. In the meantime, shields up."

"Yes, Captain."

Solaris was watching the red blip on the screen. "They're approaching alarmingly fast, Captain. I think they suspect we're about to jump. We're out of time."

"Alternatives?"

Solaris shook his head. "They have guns. Big EMP cannons and hull-piercing blasters. Military-grade. Oh, and a gun turret."

"Pirates."

"Nope. The flying pattern suggests Unity. Doesn't look like private security, either."

Rance didn't know whether to be relieved or terrified. Pirates were bad. But Unity could detain them without much reason, and that would present a whole other problem to the fugitives onboard. Namely, herself and Solaris. "What's Unity doing all the way out here?"

"I wondered that too. Harper," Solaris called. "Did you disguise the *Streaker's* registration before we left Ares?"

"Of course, sir. Sending up our new name right now."

Suddenly, the ship-to-ship comm went live, and a man's voice rang out over the ship-wide speakers. "Star cruiser, this is Unity Alpha Class X3458, designation *Malta*. State your condition and destination."

Rance punched a button on the comm and read the name Harper sent up to her. "Hello, *Malta*. This is the *Stanley Alto*. We're on our way to pick up cargo on Noko before heading to Prometheus."

Solaris exchanged glances with Rance and mouthed, *Stanley Alto*?

She shrugged. Any other time, it would have been funny. Right now, a knot was growing in her stomach like some twisted vagrappe had taken root there.

"I'm Lieutenant Arnold," the other man said. "Nice ship. You're a bit small to be running cargo, aren't you?"

"Thank you, Lieutenant. I'm Captain Cooper. We are a private ferry. Our cargo is human. Usually paid transport."

"Oh?"

"Yes, sir. Sending you our registration."

Solaris sent it to the *Malta*, and Rance fidgeted, braiding her hair and unbraiding it. They'd never tested their new registration codes against the Unity database. She hoped it worked better than Deliverance had.

The cockpit felt suddenly warm as if the ventilation system had failed. Rance checked it, but it was fine. She was only sweating out of nervousness, nothing else.

"Had some trouble?" Arnold asked.

"We had a hyperdrive malfunction. But we're up and running now. We'll be on our way if you don't object."

"Stand by, *Stanley*."

"What do they want?" James asked nervously.

Rance glanced at Solaris, who remained calm and stoic. While she'd been busy watching the screens, he'd changed his face to sharp features and dark hair. His fun-loving persona had disappeared, replaced by a grim countenance.

"Wish I could change my face right now," she whispered.

"I can change yours for you," he said, smiling to ease the tension.

"You can?"

"Sure. What would you like to look like?"

The Lieutenant returned. "*Stanley Alto,* you are required to submit to a random inspection. Lower your shields and prepare for boarding."

"Ah, *Malta,* you're welcome, of course, but I have a group of passengers waiting for us on Noko. If we don't pick them up, someone else will. I'll lose business."

"Not my problem, Captain Cooper. Lower your shields."

"What do you want to do?" James asked. "I could make the jump. They don't have tractor beams on those Alpha Classes."

"I don't recommend it, Captain," Solaris said. "Remember when I told you Unity had ships that could follow you into hyperspace?"

"Yes?"

Solaris nodded to the red blip on his screen. It was slowing now, in anticipation of boarding them. "That's one of them."

"Of all the luck," Rance breathed harshly. "Triton's hairy backside, sometimes I hate Unity."

"That makes two of us."

Rance spoke to the crew at large. "Alright, prepare for inspection. You all know what to do. James, make sure they don't punch a hole in the cargo bay doors. Make sure they use the airlock."

There was a faint scramble as the crew left their places. Solaris looked confused. But then, he'd never been on the receiving end of an inspection before. Rance had.

"We have a few protocols for this sort of thing," she explained. "First, we do a quick sweep to make sure there's no offensive cargo in plain sight. This is easy because right now we have none."

Rance stood and walked over to the ladder. At least her toe looked better. The meds were kicking in. But she was still going to have to force it into a pair of boots.

Solaris followed her down the ladder and through the top level.

"Second," she said when she reached her own quarters, "we pretend to be the most law-abiding citizens in the empire."

"Now I know you're insane," he said. "There is such a thing as looking too perfect."

Rance entered her cabin and grabbed her boots—not the magnetic ones. She eased her foot into the first one. When it didn't hurt, she hurriedly put on the second. "These guys tend to get bored and restless. Not much action out here in the DEEP unless they get lucky and find pirates. They're just itching to arrest somebody and haul them to the nearest Triton-controlled planet or waystation. So, we don't give them any reason."

"Sounds like you've already done this a few times."

Rance shot Solaris a look as she eased back out the door.

"Captain? How many times?"

"Once."

Surprised, Solaris stopped in his tracks. "Really? You're basing your plan of action on one incident?"

"It's not the worst plan. What else should we do? Rush to tell them about all the illegal operations we've completed? Give up the names of all the contacts we've made this side of the Nilurian Belt? Or maybe tell them your real name, or *mine* for that matter."

"I was merely suggesting you have a bit better cover."

"We don't need it. We're nobodies. And I try to keep it that way, *Roote*. Now, are you ready?"

Solaris looked torn, like he had something on his mind but didn't want to say it.

"What?" she asked as they descended the stairs.

He shook his head.

"*Stanley Alto*," the officer said, "make sure all crew is present and accounted for when we arrive."

Rance pressed a button on her handset. "Ready and waiting, Lieutenant. I ought to warn you—only one of you can fit through at a time. Sorry about that. It's on the list of upgrades I'd like to make."

The comm was silent.

"You've scared them, boss," Abel said seriously. "They don't want to walk into an ambush. Using that airlock, we could pick them off one by one if we wanted to."

"If that were the plan, Abel, I wouldn't have told them about the airlock."

"Unless they suspected you were lying to make them let their guards down," James said.

Tally shook his head in rebuke.

"What?" James asked. "I wasn't trying to be funny."

The airlock hissed open, and an armored soldier entered the inner chamber and waited for it to close. He watched them through the tiny porthole, his face obscured by his lowered visor.

"Don't try anything funny, *Stanley*," the lieutenant said over the comm.

James snorted.

"Our guys are going to signal when they're over safely. If they don't, we're going to blast your ship all the way to the Belt."

"That's all?" Rance asked.

Tally glared at her cheekiness. James smirked. Solaris looked worried, as did Harper. Only Abel remained neutral-looking like an inspection was all part of a days' work. Few things ever bothered him. He'd been more upset about Solaris' joke about eating Henry.

Rance tried to follow suit and stay calm, but couldn't help feeling irritated at Unity's intrusion. After their delays, all she wanted to do was reach Prometheus without anything else going wrong.

The first soldier stood inside the tiny airlock, waiting for the pressure to equalize. With his armor, he barely fit.

This inspection wouldn't take long. The *Star Streaker* was a small ship. The few secret panels under the hold and in engineering were accessible only by a secret passcode tapped in the exact right location. Even if the Unity soldiers could open the hatches, they didn't have anything inside them on this trip. Rance only had to hold her tongue for a few minutes. And stay calm.

But facing down Unity was different from facing down pirates. She considered both and decided she'd rather go with pirates. At least pirates couldn't take her back to her father.

"Harper, what'd you do with that problem drive?" Rance

whispered, referring to the Caducean Drive that held Deliverance.

"Stowed carefully where no one will find her, Captain."

Rance nodded in relief. If Harper hid it, even Rance might not be able to find it unless she took the ship apart. She trusted her crew completely. They joked and quarreled like siblings, but in the end, they were her family. And she trusted each one of them with her life.

The airlock really needed an upgrade. Rance had been staring at that helmeted soldier for two whole minutes.

Finally, the light over the door turned green, and the soldier squeezed through. He stood tall in his black armor, as tall as Rance. The standard-issue armor carried Unity's insignia on the breastplate—a trident, a hammer, and a sparrow. The three emblems of the separate armies that had formed the original military force of Triton.

In the beginning, the Empire Triton had been an alliance only. Now, the separate ruling entities had melded into one big conglomerate under one command—the Emperor Supreme. He controlled Unity, the largest single military force in the history of mankind.

The door hissed closed, and the soldier looked around at the crew. They stood as non-threateningly as they could, with their hands relaxed at their sides.

He fixed his gaze on Solaris.

Did he recognize him somehow? Or was he just surprised at his height? Solaris always looked too big, even in the hold where the ceiling was taller.

The black soldier studied him a minute, then swept his eyes across to Rance. He paused. Rance's heart beat faster. She tried to calm down, knowing he was probably reading her vital signs with the sensors in his helmet. But her body was rebelling. Her hand wanted to fidget. She forced it to remain still.

No one said anything, and the drawn-out silence became awkward.

To take her mind off the soldier's scrutiny, Rance focused on using her ZOD to study his armor. It was good—even the patrols out in the DEEP got regular upgrades. Strong, nearly seamless joints, weapons attachments on every appendage, even the gauntlet, which looked like it could extend claw-like razor blades from each finger.

Ignoring the battle-ready armor and the other soldier waiting in the airlock, Rance swallowed her anxiety and stepped forward.

"Inspection's over," she said, adopting her most commanding tone. "At least of my crew. You are welcome to look around the ship, but we are on a tight schedule."

"Are you the captain?" the soldier asked.

"I'm Captain Cooper," she said. "This is my ship. You'll find the registration is in order. Will any more of you be joining us?"

The next soldier came through the inner door of the airlock and closed it behind him. Then, he turned to the crew. His darkened visor turned straight to Rance. Since she couldn't see his face, it made his silence worse. Not being able to read the soldiers' facial expressions was putting her at a disadvantage.

The second soldier stepped forward, stopped, and faced Rance. Then, he tilted his head a degree to the side, as if in surprise.

"Devri?" he asked.

Rance's blood ran cold, and a shiver traveled down her spine. How did that soldier know her real name? After all, she didn't look much like Devri anymore. Only someone who'd known her well would even recognize her. Why, *why* hadn't she taken Solaris up on his offer to change her face too?

In a split-second decision, Rance decided the best course of action was to play dumb.

"Who?" she asked.

The soldier flipped a latch on his helmet and pulled it off his head. His short, dark hair was slicked back, his features brown, like someone who was a native of Xanthes. Rance's heart sank to her knees. Playing dumb wouldn't work with this one.

"Hello, Devri," he said. "You have to remember me."

Rance sighed. "Hello, Turkey."

Beside her, James raised an eyebrow. Rance ignored him.

Turkey smiled. "So you do remember. How long has it been?"

"Ummm, Captain?" Harper asked.

"Six or seven years, I think," Rance said. She looked at Harper. "This is Alaster Arnold—we always called him Turkey at the Xanthes Flight Academy. Although I guess we should call him Lieutenant now."

Of course, someone from the XFA would recognize her, better than her Noble friends. At the Academy, Rance had looked much like she did now. No make-up, hair pulled back, flight suit. What were the odds she'd run into someone she knew out here?

The game was up. She might as well let them put her in energy cuffs right now.

"I heard you'd left that dustball rock we called home," the lieutenant said. He nodded to the other soldier who took off into the galley and lower level, beginning his inspection.

Turkey approached Rance. The crew stiffened, all of them alert to a possible attack.

"I also heard about why you left," Turkey said quietly.

"Turkey—"

He held up his hand to cut off Rance's plea, and looked at the others, aware of their proximity and their dour expressions. But none of them would be a match for the lieutenant in his armor, except maybe Solaris. An image of Solaris fighting armored soldiers on Doxor 5 sprang to Rance's mind. He had taken them out with ease then. But if he were to fight, he'd give away his identity.

Too bad Abel hadn't donned his armor, but he'd left it off in the interest of looking *cooperative*. No, fighting wasn't their best option right now.

Rance had got the distinct impression Turkey was trying not to talk too much while the other soldier was close, and a small ray of hope ran through her. She shook off her fear and looked Turkey straight in the eye.

"What are you going to do?"

She never liked orbiting a topic when she could land right on it.

Turkey seemed to decide Abel was the biggest threat and kept one eye on him as he addressed Rance.

"You do know there's an exorbitant reward out for your return to your father?"

James scoffed. "Listen, Lieutenant."

Tally shook his head at James in warning. Turkey saw the gesture and stared at Tally. "I know who you are too."

"Look at me," Rance said, drawing his gaze away from her friends. "I'm the captain. What are you going to do?"

There was no love lost between Rance and Turkey. Even though he'd been a year ahead of her, they'd been rivals in the XFA competitions. In rival Houses, on rival teams. He had been good, not great. But he was a favorite among his superiors because he always toed the line. With Turkey, rules were rules. Rance hoped he'd changed.

"What I'm supposed to do," Turkey said finally as if he were offended she'd even asked. "Not only is there a reward, but all of Unity is under strict orders to arrest you on sight."

That answered her question. He was still the same when it came to rules. "And yet I notice you haven't commed your captain and escorted me to the brig on your ship."

Turkey shook his head. "Not the brig, a secure cabin. We'd be blasted into the Razor Nebula if we put Davos' daughter in the brig."

"Alright, that's enough," Solaris said. The talk of putting Rance in the brig had finally made him burst. "The captain is not going anywhere with you."

"And you are?"

"My name is Roote. I'm the CO aboard this ship, and you've made a grave error, Lieutenant."

Turkey smiled. "Have I? Do you know who your captain is?"

A bead of sweat ran down Rance's back. How would they get out of this? She tried to remember something—anything— to use against Turkey. He'd come from a poor family, she remembered. With all that talk of the reward, he seemed motivated by money.

And then she had an idea. She glanced back at the galley where the other soldier had disappeared. "Lieutenant, can I talk to you in private?"

"If you think you're going to change my mind—"

Rance shook her head. "No, but I think there's something you need to be aware of."

Without waiting for an answer, Rance turned and climbed the stair to the top level. The only place they could get privacy would be the cockpit. When Turkey made to follow her, Solaris, James, and Abel all headed for the stairs, like they meant to go too.

Rance turned to them. "I said, in *private*. Stay here."

"Captain," James warned.

Rance glared him into silence. "I'll call you if you're needed. This way, Lieutenant."

He followed her all the way to the cockpit. He was barely able to fit up the ladder in his armor, and no way was he sitting down. That was okay. Rance didn't want to sit, anyway.

He angled himself where he could see the hatch as if he anticipated a double-cross of some kind.

"Look," Rance began without preamble. "Is there anything I can say that would make you let me go? As in, *poof*, we just disappeared?"

Turkey laughed. "No. Why don't you want to go back to your father?"

Rance shot him a disgusted look and then remembered she was going to be civilized with him.

"If it's about the money," she said. "I can figure out a way to get it to you."

"I doubt it. You have ten million credits hiding out in a bank somewhere?"

Rance gaped at him, choking over the amount. When had the reward for her arrest gone so high?

"Come on, Devri. Go quietly, and maybe we'll be lenient to your crew."

Another cold shiver ran down Rance's back. "What do you mean?"

"They're involved too. Aiding and abetting."

Rance snorted. "That's not right, and you know it. I'm the captain of this ship. They're only here for the paycheck."

"I doubt that. They have willingly helped you. The frightened looks on their faces when I said your real name told me all I needed to know. They weren't surprised. They were worried about you. Still, their loyalty is admirable. Stupid, but admirable."

"I can get you something else. Not money."

"There's nothing you can say that will persuade me. And you don't have anything of value anyway, except this ship. I can't very well take that, can I?"

Rance's mouth went dry. "What's going to happen to the ship?"

"We can't tow it, that's certain. It's a long haul back to Xanthes."

"You'll take me straight back to Xanthes?!"

"Where else would we take you?"

"And you'll just leave the ship here, drifting out in the DEEP?" Rance pictured the *Streaker* drifting forlornly out in space, abandoned and unprotected. If pirates didn't get it, some tow would. And it would be sold to the highest bidder at auction.

"We'll send a salvage crew to pick it up," he said, confirming Rance's fear.

"A salvage crew?" Rance groaned. "NO. Turkey, the ship is mine."

"Sorry, Devri." He almost looked like he meant it.

Turkey gestured to the hatch and the ladder, indicating that the conversation was over.

Desperate, Rance pulled out her last trick. She took a deep breath to steady her nerves, and said, "I have a Caducean Drive."

Turkey pulled up. "What?"

"A Caducean Drive. An imperial AI."

"I know what it is," he said sharply. "What are you doing with it?"

"I stumbled across it."

"Who stumbles across a Caducean Drive?" he asked, his eyes narrowing in suspicion and mistrust.

"You'd be surprised," Rance muttered. Then she added, "You can take it. I'm sure the empire is asking a bigger reward for it than Davos is for me. Take it and forget you saw me."

"What's stopping me from taking both of you?"

"Because you'd never find it."

"I will if I take the ship apart."

Rance rolled her eyes. She really needed to stop doing that. "It's not *here*. Do you think I'm stupid?"

Turkey looked at her dubiously. He didn't believe her.

"This is serious, Devri. It's no longer a charge of running out on a Founders' marriage. You'd be in possession of stolen imperial goods, not to mention that this a horrendous breach of security."

Rance blew out a breath of frustration. Apparently, Turkey hadn't changed much at all. Still the law-abiding, rigid person he'd always been. She wished she hadn't said anything. Now, she might be in bigger trouble. And what would that mean for her crew?

Turkey pulled out a small device the size of a coin and slapped it on Rance's right wrist. A silver substance shot out of it, wrapping around her wrist.

"Hold out your other hand," he commanded.

Rance hesitated. This was *not* happening. How had she let it get this far? Why hadn't they fought them off?

Irritated at Rance's refusal to cooperate, Turkey grabbed her other wrist. She jerked her arm, but his gauntleted hand held her tightly. The silver shot out, wrapping itself around both wrists. Then, it glowed white, sealing to her skin with an uncomfortable, burning cold. An energy cuff.

"How do you expect me to get down the ladder?" she asked snidely, her cordiality slipping in the face of becoming a prisoner. "If I slip and break a leg, you'll have my father to answer to."

"I'll risk it," he said. Then, he pulled her—not harshly despite his words—toward the hatch. Rance turned and found her footing. Her toe barely ached anymore, and she was grateful she didn't have to hop down the ladder on one foot, hands cuffed so that she could only hang onto one rung at a time.

Turkey jumped down as soon as she reached the bottom, cutting off any thought she had of running to her cabin and locking the door. It wouldn't have done any good, anyway. He would have simply burst through.

When they reached the stairway to the hold, the crew was standing at the base, anxiously watching them descend. The other soldier stood off the side, staring toward the airlock.

That was odd. He wasn't even watching the crew.

Solaris' face looked grim, grimmer even with his dark hair and sharp features. He watched Rance descend, utterly unconcerned about the armed soldier at his back.

Something was up. Solaris would never ignore an enemy at his back. Rance shot him a puzzled look, but he didn't return it. When she reached the bottom, she moved aside to let Turkey off the stair. She turned.

Turkey stood at the top of the stair, gazing at the ceiling like it was the most fascinating thing he'd ever seen.

"Lieutenant?" Rance and Solaris asked together.

Rance looked at Solaris. Up close, she saw sweat breaking out on his face. A kind of energy emanated from him, along with a metallic tang that swept through the air surrounding him.

Turkey looked at him too.

"Lieutenant," Solaris said smoothy, "did you find anything of interest?"

Turkey struggled a moment, confusion playing out across his face. Finally, he said, "There was something, but it's gone now."

He looked at Rance, his now-dull eyes no longer flickering with recognition.

Rance frowned at Solaris. What was he doing?

Turkey descended the stairs and halted in front of

Solaris. His gaze flickered back to Rance and then to his buddy.

"We need the key," Rance whispered, holding up her cuffed hands.

To her surprise, Turkey pulled a key out of a tiny compartment on his armor. He unlocked her cuffs by tapping the disc and put them back in their place on his belt.

"Thank you for your inspection, Lieutenant," Solaris said. "Say goodbye now."

"Goodbye," Turkey said, smiling stupidly. And then he marched to the airlock, signaling the other soldier as he went.

Since the airlock was still slow, and they could only go one at a time, Turkey ended up standing in the hold far longer than Rance would have liked. The rest of the crew remained mute, the silence stretching out awkwardly while they waited for both soldiers to leave.

When Turkey had left through the walkway attaching the two ships, the *Malta* detached from the *Star Streaker* and pulled away.

"What was that?" Rance said, rounding on Solaris.

He shrugged. "Just a little trick I picked up while evading pirates."

"That's not a good answer."

"It'll have to do," he said, nodding toward the airlock. "We have about five more minutes before they come to their senses and try to board us again. Better get out of here."

Rance hurried up the stairs with James and Solaris following. The rest of the crew scattered to find their places.

"Why do I feel you're always evading my questions, Solaris?" Rance asked.

"Not evading, Captain. You always ask them at the worst times."

Rance rolled her eyes before she remembered she wasn't going to do that anymore.

They climbed into the cockpit and took their places. By the time they'd harnessed in, Harper had already sent jump coordinates to Rance's console. James flipped switches and buttons and placed a steady hand on the throttle.

A voice came over the comm. "*Stanley Alto*, you will submit to a random inspection."

The crew of the *Malta* was still confused. Rance hoped it was enough to stop them from following the *Streaker* into hyperspace.

"Punch it, James," Rance said.

James didn't need to be told again. The stars shifted, black turned to blue, and they made the jump.

Rance watched the radar for signs of being followed.

"They didn't follow us," Solaris said.

"Are you sure?"

"Reasonably."

"That's comforting," James shot over his shoulder.

When Rance looked at Solaris, he'd changed back into his normal face.

"Next time," she said wearily, "just disguise us all."

"Let's hope there won't be a next time. How's the toe?"

She waved away the question. "Don't change the subject."

"What subject?"

"How you confused them."

"Ah," Solaris said, smirking. "Again, it has to do with

altering their perception of the way things are. I made our ship look like their own."

"It looked the same as always to me."

"But they saw their own cargo bay. It confused them enough that their minds couldn't keep up. Caused that dazed look you saw."

"So you can alter others' perception of their surroundings?"

"I do it all the time when I change my face. Does it bother you?"

"It's a bit unsettling."

"A bit?" James asked, putting the *Streaker* on autopilot and swiveling his chair around to look at them. "It's like marching into Hades blind. Solaris, *no one* likes the idea of you being able to manipulate them like that."

Solaris looked disgruntled. "It never bothered you before, when I was *saving your life*."

He looked to Rance for help, but she was feeling uncomfortable by the whole thing as well.

"I would never use it against you," he said, looking into her eyes. He flicked his gaze to James, who was still scowling. "James, yes, but never you, Captain."

"How would we know?"

"Oh trust me, you'd know. When you come out of the daze, you remember pretty much everything."

The sinking feeling returned. Rance unbuckled her harness and stood, planning to go back to bed. The day had been too stressful already.

"Captain," Solaris whispered. "What did you say to the Lieutenant?"

"When?"

"When you asked to speak to him privately."

Solaris looked anxious, his eyes holding something like fear. Rance had never seen that expression on his face before, and it puzzled her.

"I offered him the Caducean Drive," she said.

Solaris raised both eyebrows in surprise.

James choked out, "What?"

"I didn't have an option. I thought I could blackmail him. Solaris, do you think he'll remember?"

Solaris took a deep breath and ran a hand through his hair. For some reason, he looked relieved. "Probably."

"Then this is terrible," she said. "Why are you smiling?"

Solaris tried to straighten his face. "I thought, maybe, you were going to give me away."

"What?!" Rance shouted. "How could you think that?"

James shook his head and whispered, "Wrong thing to say, man."

If Rance had felt a sinking feeling before, it was nothing to the cold water that had been dumped on her now. How could Solaris think that? After all they'd been through? She didn't give up her friends. They were family. *He* was family. All she had.

Tears stung her eyes for the second time that day, but she preferred the pain of a broken toe to the pain in her chest. Rance hurried down the ladder, practically sliding down it and going to her cabin.

She heard Solaris on the ladder behind her. Then, James' voice carried down through the hatch. "Better leave her alone. You'll only make it worse."

Rance was grateful James knew her moods, and thankful

that Solaris seemed to understand this. He didn't follow her as she stalked into her cabin and closed the door.

She wasn't angry but hurt. Did Solaris really think she would give him up to the empire at the first real sign of trouble? Her chest ached, her toe throbbed again as she removed her boots, and it all sent her into a depressing spin. Rance flopped back, staring at the ceiling.

She refused to think about Turkey, or how close she'd come to being carried away to Xanthes. Rance would never see Turkey again, probably. The empire was a big place after all. But she couldn't help but feel uneasy about being recognized. And opening her big fat mouth about the Caducean Drive. Something told her that lapse in judgment would come back to haunt her one day.

Remembering Henry, Rance sat up again and checked everything. Satisfied the little nuisance wasn't anywhere around, she lay back down and pulled a blanket over her head. She didn't think she could deal with any more mishaps today. Rance waved her hand, and the cabin lights went out.

CHAPTER FOUR

Rance woke to find a tiny finger stuck up her left nostril. On the verge of panic, she thought she was suffocating before she heard Henry's contented trills next to her on the pillow. This time, she pushed him away instead of throwing him across the room. Henry fell off the bed with a soft thump and squeaked excitedly at her.

"You had that coming. Now get out. Go find Solaris and bug him."

But then she remembered the door was closed. She dragged herself out of bed and opened it. The corridor was dark, the ship back on night cycle. How long had she been asleep?

"How did you get in here?" she asked Henry.

James happened to be passing on his nightly check of the ship's instruments.

"I'm not in there, Captain," he said with a smirk. "One of the rules, remember?"

"Oh shut up, James. And keep this *thing* out of my room. I swear he's trying to kill me."

James picked up Henry, who snuggled into the crook of his arm. "He was just trying to find a quiet place to sleep, weren't you Henry? Bad Captain Rance isn't very nice."

"Everything quiet?"

"Perfect. No hiccups."

Rance huffed, stepped back into her room, and shut the door. Then she locked it for good measure.

Despite her weariness, all traces of sleep had vanished. She tossed and turned, trying to erase the worry in her mind.

Rance told herself the uneasy feeling in her gut was just excitement. After the *Streaker's* breakdown, Rance was attuned to every noise, every clunk, every distant clamor. All of them were normal, none of them made her feel better.

They hadn't been on any real jobs in months, nor had she been to Prometheus in almost ten years. The anticipation was spilling over and making her nervous. That's all it was. She needed to relax. They were on their way again, with a simple mission ahead of them.

"I don't think there's anything wrong with being nervous," Solaris told her the next day. "In fact, it shows you have some sense."

"And you doubted me before?" she asked. They were both determinedly pretending like nothing had happened the day before. Solaris wisely didn't repeat his concern, and Rance, although still affronted that he'd thought she would turn him in, realized he'd been under stress too. His fear was logical.

Maybe. They'd talk about it later. Right now, she just wanted a day of peace and quiet.

Solaris sat down across from her in the galley with two more cups of Harper's tea. He had made this batch. He slid one cup across the table to Rance. The tea had been the crew's supper since they left Ares, that and the dehydrated rations Abel had found stashed in a cupboard in his room. They were very old and barely enough to keep everyone from turning to cannibalism.

Rance took a sip of tea and grimaced.

"Not good?"

"Let's just say it isn't as good as Harper's." She took another sip anyway, then gagged. "Triton's fingernail, what'd you put in this, Solaris?"

Solaris shrugged. "Extra leaves."

"It tastes like mud." She set the cup back down, pushing it away in disgust.

Solaris narrowed his eyes. "Have you ever tasted mud, your Ladyship?"

"None of that."

Something grunted behind Solaris, and they both turned toward the empty pantry. Henry had climbed up the refrigerated storage units and was now dangling from a metal handle. His little arms reached for the next one. When he caught it, he swung across the units like he was swinging from branch to branch on a tree.

"So much for staying with Harper and Abel," Rance said in irritation. She knew that wouldn't last.

Solaris twitched his nose as if he were trying not to sneeze. But it seemed that if Henry stayed out of arm's reach, Solaris was fine.

He turned away from the cappatter and leaned forward. "Meeting your old friend was a surprise, yesterday, huh?"

"He's not really a friend, especially since he was going to turn me over to my father. *Friends don't do things like that.*"

Okay, maybe they were going to talk about this today.

"Aren't we friends, Solaris?"

Solaris raised an eyebrow, "Yes."

"Then why'd you think I would betray you? I don't leave my team behind, and I certainly don't turn them over to the authorities. I expect the same from you. You wouldn't, would you?"

Solaris looked alarmed. "Of course not. But would you turn over your friend if you knew they'd done something truly heinous?"

Rance's interest piqued, and she forgot her foul mood. What had kind, good-natured Solaris done that he'd considered *heinous*?

"Like what?" she asked.

Solaris waved her away. "Nothing in particular, just asking."

Rance didn't quite believe him. "Why would you bring it up then? Honestly, Solaris, sometimes I really don't get you."

"The feeling is mutual."

They sat in awkward silence a moment, Rance looking at her tea and wishing it was more palatable, and wondering how they'd started quarreling again.

"So," she said finally. "Ask me something then."

"Huh?"

"A very intelligent question—*huh*," Rance teased. She smiled, trying to ease the tension.

Solaris smiled back. "You don't want me to start asking questions."

Rance shrugged. There wasn't much he could ask that would bother her.

"Okay, then," he said, taking up the challenge. "I'm curious. And running into your friend Turkey yesterday made me wonder. What's it like going from someone like Moira or Devri to Rance Cooper, daring smuggler and Captain extraordinaire?"

Rance crossed her arms and gave Solaris a shrewd look. His open, honest face was quirked into something between amusement and curiosity.

"Do you really want to know?"

"Yes."

Rance smirked. "I was never like Moira, so your question doesn't apply. But the change isn't something I think about much. I'm still Devri."

"And Rance."

"Yes, why?"

"No reason." Solaris drummed his hands on the table and looked around the galley as if food would magically materialize on the shelves.

"Tell me."

His eyes flicked back to hers. "It's a personal question."

"I assure you, everyone else on this ship knows my story. It's not a secret. I'm surprised you haven't asked sooner."

"Alright, Captain, I'll ask. You say you aren't different, but we both know that's wishful thinking. If anything, you've changed for the better. Now you know what hardship is." Then he smiled and looked around. "Well, as hard as it is to own a beautiful ship and fly it wherever in the galaxy you please."

"I don't know anything about you, Solaris, not really. But

I know that *you* know how hard it is to go from place to place, wondering if Unity is waiting to nab you at the first opportunity."

He nodded. "I do."

"Then why do you get to be all high and mighty?"

At her tone, a look of surprise crossed Solaris' face. "I must have hit a little too close to home, huh? Look, Captain —Rance—"

"Captain," she said a little too forcefully. He'd irritated her again, and she didn't feel like indulging his attempt to be friendly.

"Captain. You told me to ask, so I did. I was merely trying to pin down how you felt about the shift from a life of privilege to a life of, well, *less* privileged. You're hardly a beggar."

"I never said I was."

"Okay. But you blew it off like it was nothing. And I think it's something."

"Your thoughts are noted."

In truth, Solaris had touched on a sensitive subject. Although Rance had opened herself up for questions, his astute approach had caught her off-guard.

"So you're not going to answer the question?"

Rance sighed and sagged her shoulders in defeat. "We all like to think we're the same person, but in reality, even if my father called off the marriage and invited me back home to live as I pleased, I couldn't do it."

"And why does that irritate you?"

She looked at him shrewdly. "Those Wizard interrogation skills come in handy, don't they?"

Solaris held up his hands. "Don't answer, then."

They sat again in awkward silence, Rance staring into her

undrinkable tea and wishing it were vagrappes or lantess or even a hunk of stale bread. A lack of food had lowered her tolerance for personal questions, it seemed.

"Why can't you *magic* us some food?" she asked after a bit.

Solaris sighed into his own tea and said, "Regretfully, it doesn't work like that. Galaxy Wizards can't make something from nothing."

He took a long swig of tea and fought the urge to spew it back out. Rance almost laughed and then thought better of it. She didn't want another argument. Solaris was just as hungry as she.

"I just want to get to Prometheus, find my friend, and get out," she said after he'd managed to swallow the muddy liquid. "That hiccup yesterday with Unity was a freak occurrence. We shouldn't have any more trouble."

Solaris frowned. "Are you trying to convince yourself or me?"

"Both."

"What's the plan if we can't contact Moira?"

"We'll get in touch with her. She's expecting us—I hope. Do you think I made the wrong choice in telling Turkey about the Caducean Drive?"

Solaris sighed and looked at his empty tea cup. "Maybe. You really don't want to be Devri? And all the perks that go with it? It sounds like your family would welcome you with open arms. Is the situation that bad that you can't go back?"

"You think I should submit to an arranged marriage?"

"Heh. No. But I wonder why you have had such a strong reaction. Most Nobles have arranged marriages. You would have grown up expecting it."

"You've met Harrison McConnell."

Solaris smirked. "I have."

"I'm glad the prospect of me marrying him amuses one of us."

Solaris looked up at her, his expression inscrutable. "I don't think it's amusing."

"And I'm different from other Nobles, Solaris. I don't care about wealth or power. I grew up expecting different things to happen to me."

"Like meeting me," he said, smiling.

"Are you fishing for a compliment?"

"I'm open to one, yes. After all, I *did* save you from Unity's clutches yesterday."

"Yes. Thank you." Rance meant it.

Solaris held her gaze again and then said sincerely, "You're welcome. I couldn't have them running off with you."

Henry swung back over the refrigerators, trilling excitedly. Fine hairs dislodged from the cappatter and floated down over the table. Rance watched them, glad for an excuse to look away from Solaris. He'd been so odd the last few days. One minute, he was pushing her buttons, irritating her. The next, he was serious, unreadable, and strangely pensive.

Rance put it down to starvation.

When she looked back at Solaris, the moment had passed. He stood, taking her cup with his own and putting them in the sanitizer. Then, he sneezed.

In truth, Rance didn't have a plan for finding Moira if they couldn't call her. But she had a general knowledge of the section of the city her friend would be in. Rance had always liked Prometheus, mainly because it was the opposite of Xanthes. Prometheus was second only to Triton in wealth and power and looked like it. It contained one of the most advanced and beautiful residential sections in the empire, with tall glass buildings and wide-open expanses of greenery.

With everything done, the crew sat around looking at one another, thinking about their roles and how to execute the plan. Rance's stomach rumbled, and she thought the first thing she'd do before finding her friend would be to scrounge up some food. She wondered if she had anything onboard that she could bear to part with once they arrived, to buy something to eat. The Caducean Drive was out of the question. After mentioning it to Turkey and seeing his reaction, Rance vowed no one else would know they had the valuable drive onboard. Ever.

Finally, when she couldn't stand waiting any longer, Rance went to the locker down in the cargo bay and began pulling out weapons and checking them again. Solaris came out of the galley and, seeing what she was doing, joined her.

"You really are worried, aren't you?"

"Aren't you?"

"I'd be lying if I said I wasn't. But if you think this is such a bad idea, why are we going there?"

"Number one, we need the money. Number two, we need to eat. Number three, I'm curious about what's really going on, and Moira is an old friend."

Amused, Solaris raised an eyebrow at her.

Rance shot him a look. "Those things are in no particular order, of course."

Solaris' stomach picked that time to rumble. Instead of

laughing, Rance grew serious. She hoped she wasn't leading her friends into a trap, but at this point, they couldn't afford to pass up any opportunities. Until they could get back in sync with their regular contacts, she needed to find a way to take care of her crew and her ship.

"I'm sorry for the way I behaved on Ares, for getting mad about that boy," he said suddenly. "I was out of line to suggest you'd be anybody other than who you are. And I should've just let him go. And I should also apologize for thinking you'd betray me to Unity. I crossed a line. Sometimes, I still feel like I work for Unity and the Wizards. I don't have an excuse for any of it, really. But, well, I wanted you to know."

"Don't get all sentimental on me, Solaris," Rance said, offering him a blaster.

He shook his head. "I have my weapon of choice," he said, referring to his staff. "Let's hope I don't have to use it."

They both knew the consequences if Solaris used his powers. As soon as someone reported a man with uncommon power and a staff, the Galaxy Wizards would be on their way.

Rance had only seen Solaris in action once, during the incident on Doxor 5. The way he'd tricked Turkey and his buddy to leave the *Streaker* was proof he had more tricks to use. She had a feeling Solaris was hiding some very impressive moves beneath his façade of swearing off violence. Suddenly, Rance felt bad about not accepting his apology.

"What did you really do as a Galaxy Wizard? To make them hunt you like they are?"

Solaris closed the locker door, using the moment to take his eyes away from her. "More than I care to tell you about."

His voice was oddly tight like someone was squeezing his vocal cords.

"You know that just makes me more curious, right?"

Solaris looked back at her, his expression composed once again. "It's more than my life's worth to share those secrets with you or anybody for that matter."

"But you don't work for them anymore."

"Right. Which is why it would be really smart of me to stay out of anything to do with the Wizards."

"Are you still going to disguise the ship when we get to Prometheus?"

"Of course."

"Just checking."

Just then, an ear-splitting howl came from engineering.

"What in Triton's name is that?" Solaris asked.

"That's Tally!"

When they got to him, Tally was in a battle with Henry, who was sitting atop the Graeken's ridge, tiny fangs dug into his head. Green drops of blood ran down Tally's head and face.

"What happened?" Rance asked as she hurried over.

Tally spun around, grabbing hold of Henry and attempting to pull him off. But the creature had burrowed himself into Tally's head like a tick attaches to a dog.

"Get him off!" Tally yelled.

Rance grabbed hold of Henry while Solaris grabbed the cappatter's arms. Henry took his fangs out of Tally and hissed, the white fangs green with Tally's blood. Also, Henry had retractable claws, which he extended when Solaris tried to pry him off.

Finally, after getting scratched themselves, Rance and

Solaris managed to get Henry away from Tally. The Graeken held his head and fumed.

"I found him in one of the engine housings! When I tried to get him out, he attacked!"

Solaris sneezed and quickly let go of Henry. The animal wrapped itself around Rance's arms and hissed at Tally again. The little thing quivered in fear.

"You scared him, Tally," she said.

"*I* scared *him*? Does anyone on this ship have any sense?" He looked from Rance to Solaris.

"I guess we know why someone was going to throw him in the river," Solaris said. "Those things aren't supposed to have fangs and claws. It's a mutant."

Rance shushed the furry creature in her hands and said, "We need a box for him to stay in when he's not being watched."

"We need a box, alright," Tally said, dabbing his bleeding head with a rag. "For its burial."

"I think you better have Harper look at your head," Solaris told him, sneezing again.

With much grumbling and a lot of dirty looks at Henry, Tally allowed them to escort him across the hold to the med bay. Harper came out of the control room to dab Tally's wounds with ointment. The ridge on his head was made of bone, so Henry's claws hadn't damaged anything more than Tally's scales.

After seeing Harper was going to fix him up, Rance turned to go.

"Captain," Tally said as Harper pulled out a scanner and did a quick full-body check for other injuries. "Can I have a word with you?"

Henry hopped out of Rance's hands and rolled out of the med bay. "If it's about Henry," she said, "I agree he's a pest."

She ignored Harper's hurt look.

"No, Captain, it's not about Henry," he said.

Harper finished by sealing Tally's torn scales with a laser. The process took two minutes.

"All better?" she asked when she finished.

Tally reached up and touched the wounds. "Yes. As always—beautiful work. Is there anything you can't do?"

Harper's cheeks turned pink. "Plenty. And you're making too much of it. Anyone can turn on this machine and follow the instructions."

"After having lived as long as I have, Harper, I doubt just *anyone* could. But I can say with all sincerity that you are a talented young woman."

Tally never spoke to the crew of his role as a servant in Rance's house. Harper didn't know he'd worked for her father Davos for years, or that he'd helped Rance run away. Even if Harper had, she couldn't have looked more pleased at his compliment.

After Harper dismissed herself, Rance shut the door and looked at Tally. He rarely asked to speak to her in private. Usually, he spoke his mind in front of the crew.

"Captain, I'm worried about going to Prometheus."

"I thought we had it all settled, Tally. You're going to stay on the ship where no one will recognize you."

"With all due respect, I'm not worried about myself, and you know it."

Rance sighed and leaned against the wall. "What would you have me do? Cancel the hyperspace jump and run away?"

"It's not about running away. It's about staying out of trouble. I'm worried about this one, Captain."

Tally's confession surprised Rance. He often hid his worry beneath a scowl or a dismissive wave. But he rarely voiced his concerns in such a serious manner.

"I'm worried about it too," she admitted. "But I think it's the right thing to do."

"We don't know what is the right thing here."

"If Moira asked for help that I'm able to give, then that's the right thing to do."

Tally took a deep breath and stared at Rance intently with his large green eyes. "I won't argue with you, but I would be remiss if I didn't ask you to reconsider."

"I have reconsidered. My decision is final."

He nodded. "Okay, then I will support you from the ship. James, Harper, and I will provide tactical help. But if you get into trouble, we're coming to get you."

Rance pushed off the wall. "Thank you, Tally."

The next evening, Rance walked around the ship with a makeshift box in her hand. Henry had caused trouble all day. He kept popping up everywhere, and so did his fur. Fine, ginger hairs floated around the *Star Streaker*. They drifted and settled everywhere—floors, clothes, beds, and the air return vents.

Harper had used some of it to make an antihistamine for Solaris. But everything she'd tried so far had only made him sneeze harder. Finally, he'd barricaded himself in his quarters to get away from the creature.

"Huh," James said. He stood on a small hoverboard in the corridor on the top deck, peering into the ventilation shafts. A ceiling grate lay on its side near a bulkhead.

"What?" Rance asked.

"I just figured out how Henry gets into your room, Captain. He's going through the ventilation shafts. There's a ton of hair up here."

"How's he getting inside? Even he's too big to get through those slats in the grates."

"He must be able to flatten himself out."

"All the more reason to get him into this box. If he isn't being played with or fed or watched, he has to live in here."

"Aww, Captain."

"Aww, Captain, nothing. I keep finding him in my boots. My flight suit is covered in hair, and my entire room smells like cinnamon."

"That's not terrible."

"It is terrible. He won't leave me alone."

"He likes you and Solaris best. I can't figure out why. The two of you don't like him at all."

"I just don't like him on the ship. And after his attack on Tally, maybe we shouldn't keep him. Maybe we can find a nice home for him on Prometheus."

James cast her a pitiful look. "He loves the *Streaker*! We can't abandon him on a strange planet."

Rance shook her head. "You only say that because you haven't found him pushing buttons in the cockpit."

James paled. "You found him in my cockpit?"

"Yes, about an hour ago. That's when I went to find a box and make him a crate myself. It seems no one else was going to follow orders and do it."

James hopped down off the hoverboard and sprinted to the ladder. No doubt to check the instrument panels in the cockpit.

"I'll just put this hoverboard away, shall I?" she called after him.

Rance hunted the entire ship for Henry, but no one had seen him. If he could climb through the ventilation shafts, he could get stuck up there and die. Then they'd have to take the *Streaker* apart to get him.

She hoped it wouldn't come to that.

Finally, she stowed her box down in the galley with strict instructions for Abel to keep looking. She wanted to check on their flight status.

As Rance passed Solaris' quarters, she heard a happy squeal and soft *clink*. She paused and knocked on the door.

"Solaris? Is Henry in there?"

He didn't answer, but Rance heard the unmistakable sounds of Henry swinging around the room. If Solaris were in there, he wouldn't have allowed that to continue.

Henry's hair would be everywhere, and Solaris was already sneezing all over the ship. The one place he had been hiding without problems had been his room.

Rance pushed the button at the door. It hissed open, allowing light from the corridor into the room.

Henry sat in the middle of the bed, surrounded by a pile of blankets.

"Solaris?" Rance asked one more time.

But he wasn't under the covers. Henry looked up at Rance and hummed.

"Get out of there, you little fur ball. You're going to make him miserable."

Henry held up one of his arms, and something shiny caught the light.

"What is that? Put it down." Rance glanced up and down the corridor. She didn't know where Solaris was, and he would want Henry out of there as soon as possible.

Rance stepped into his room and walked over to the bed. She'd planned on grabbing Henry and getting out, but when she saw what was in his hand, she paused. Henry held it out for her to see.

It was a ring—an intricate, heavy gold band. The top had an old-fashioned ship's sail with a slash through it. The symbol looked familiar. Rance held it up to the light to get a better look.

It was Pirate Kaur's standard. Kaur was the most feared pirate in the galaxy. She'd never seen the standard painted on a ship, thankfully, but any captain worth her salt knew what it looked like.

What was Solaris doing with this ring?

"Ahem."

Rance turned. Solaris stood in the doorway, looking irritated.

"Oh. Umm." Rance pointed to Henry. "Well, this is awkward."

"Yes. May I ask what you're doing, Captain?"

"Henry got in here. I was trying to get him out."

Solaris waved his hand at the creature. A small, transparent wave of energy shot out of it and pinged Henry. He trilled again, hopped off the bed, and scuttled out of the room.

"I've never seen you use magic without your staff, Solaris."

Solaris looked both amused and annoyed. The struggle played out over his face like he wanted to say something but couldn't decide which emotion would win out.

The ring was still in Rance's hand, and she didn't know how to give it back to him. She half-thought of trying to sneak back into his room later and replace it. Maybe she could blame Henry for its disappearance. But it looked like a personal trinket, and Rance was embarrassed she'd even touched it. The longer she stood there, the more uncomfortable he looked.

"Of course, it's your ship, Captain, and you can go anywhere you wish," Solaris said finally. "But what about the rules?"

"No companions in quarters?"

He smiled.

"I think we've established the circumstances around that one already."

"Oh? You thought I was in trouble. I see."

Rance snorted. "Next time I'll just leave Henry in here to wallow all over your bed. What do I care if you have red, puffy eyes?"

"Because I'll look like a mess. You won't want to look at me."

Rance couldn't figure out why she felt more awkward all of a sudden. She fiddled with the ring in her hand. She smiled, attempting to diffuse the tension. Solaris gave her a puzzled look and backed out of the doorway.

Rance left the room. When she reached the corridor, she turned and held the ring out to him. "Henry found this."

Solaris nodded and took it. Then he put it in his pocket.

"It's Kaau li's," he said without hesitation.

Rance raised an eyebrow in surprise. Kaau li was the smuggler who had dropped the Caducean Drive, and Deliverance, into their possession. Kaau li was also the mother of Pirate Kaur's child. Rance had suspected Solaris had a thing for the woman. But she was still embarrassed about trespassing in his quarters, so she decided not to tease him about it.

"You don't have to tell me why you have it," she said. But she hoped he would. "Unless you're a pirate. Then I need to know about that."

Solaris grinned. "Not a pirate."

"Okay."

Rance turned to leave, but her curiosity burned too hotly to just let the subject drop.

"Why *do* you have it?"

"I thought I didn't have to tell you?"

"You don't." But Rance held her breath, waiting for an answer anyway.

Solaris smirked and shook his head. "I suppose it is odd that a Galaxy Wizard would have something like that. Kaau li gave me the ring after I saved her from the Enforcers. I felt weird about telling you."

"Why?"

"Because."

Rance was about to ask more when James' voice came over the comm. "Exiting hyperspace in six hours, Captain."

Rance bristled at the interruption, but Solaris looked relieved. As she turned for the ladder into the cockpit, he sneezed.

"All right, crew," Rance called over the comm, "spend the next six hours sleeping. We've got to be fresh when we arrive.

Abel, Henry was heading down to the cargo bay. Make sure he's safe in that box. We all need some sleep."

Despite what Rance told her crew about sleeping, when she finally laid down she stayed awake a long time, staring at the dark ceiling of her cabin. Everything Solaris and Tally had told her was true. They were headed straight for an unknown, possibly dangerous situation. But she didn't feel she had any other options.

She rolled over on her side, staring at the blank wall. The ring in Solaris' room was another puzzle. After thinking about it a while longer, she decided it wasn't her business. Solaris hadn't tried to hide it. Maybe some day he'd tell her why he hadn't wanted her to know about it.

The gentle hum of the *Star Streaker* pulled Rance into an uneasy sleep. She dreamed of random things, mostly of her father searching for her, and not being able to find Moira when they landed on Prometheus. She woke when the cabin lights came on, signaling the exit from hyperspace. Rance pulled on her magnetic boots—mercifully free of Henry—braided her hair, and walked out the door.

In the cockpit, James was already strapped into his seat, hunched over the control stick.

"Five minutes, Captain."

Solaris came in right behind Rance. His hair still stuck up in the back—he must have just woken as well. Abel and Tally were in the hold, strapping into seats that folded out from the walls. Harper was in the control room.

Rance shook the last bits of sleep from her brain and commed the crew. "Remember, we're going to find Moira, bring her back to the ship, and take off again. No wandering.

No one has permission to leave the *Streaker* unless their names are Solaris, Abel, and Captain."

"Yes, Captain," the others chimed in.

Solaris glanced at Rance just as the blue haze of hyperspace washed over the ship and disappeared. She looked out the window, expecting the sparkling cities of Prometheus to reflect the light of the green star it orbited.

Instead, she saw enormous, dark Renegade ships blocking their view of everything.

Everything except more ships behind them.

Gigantic black ships, repurposed Renegades and Destroyers, blocked the view of the planet. They were armed from every side—rotating guns, hull-piercing blasters, and cannons that could blow the *Streaker* into another galaxy.

None of them were Unity ships, either. Each one had a different symbol painted on it, but all carried an additional symbol next to it—a black sail with a slash going through it. Just like the ring in Solaris' room.

"That's Pirate Kaur's standard," Solaris said calmly. He spoke as if he hadn't just revealed that the deadliest pirate in the galaxy had surrounded one of the most powerful planets in the empire.

Rance fought the urge to panic. *Now* they knew what was happening on Prometheus. Despite the shiver of fear that ran through Rance, she couldn't help but be impressed at the display of power surrounding the planet. And angry. Kaur had grown bold indeed if he thought he could swoop in and take over the second-most influential planet in the empire.

James altered course and ducked beneath the first Renegade. Through glimpses between ships, they saw numerous tiny ships had launched from Prometheus. None of the smaller spacecraft were getting through. Kaur's ships surrounded the planet like predators at a watering hole, waiting for prey.

Rance almost ordered James to turn and run. But what if Moira was stuck on the planet below, with no way to escape?

As if he was thinking the same thing, James asked, "Still want to go in, Captain?"

"Yes," she said a little too loudly. No one commented on it.

A small X-Class fighter with the slashed flag symbol dove through the herd, and the prey scattered.

Solaris looked at one of the dark ships blocking their view of Prometheus. "I didn't realize Kaur had so many ships," he said. "He's been busy."

"Where's Unity?" Rance asked. She never thought she'd wish to see the military might of Triton. But the pirates were more frightening than any Unity fighters she'd ever faced. How different she'd felt from a few days ago when she'd wished to see pirates instead of that Unity ship, the *Malta*. After seeing Kaur's standard on so many ships, though, Rance knew which one she preferred.

James turned the ship away from the planet and then glanced over his shoulder at Rance.

"What is going on?" she repeated.

"I don't know," James said. "Looks like all those little ships are trying to get out."

"Looks like it," Solaris answered. "That's why we haven't

been able to get through to your friend, Captain. They're jamming all communications off the planet."

"Are the pirates attacking the *entire* planet?"

"Looks like it," Solaris repeated grimly.

James concentrated on flying through and around the old Renegades and Destroyers. Once, these ships had been the prize of Unity. But as newer models and technology replaced them, they had been stripped down and sold to the highest bidders. Rance wondered if Unity knew it had sold its own ships to pirates.

As they entered the main mass of ships near Prometheus, they saw many of them had symbols of Noble houses.

"If they aren't letting them through," Rance said, "what will happen when we try to get out?"

James hunched over the controls, his nose inches from his flight controls. "Too late now," he said. "We've passed the last barricade."

"Solaris, I think it's about time you did some of your magic work."

Solaris frowned. "Except I don't think it will matter," he said. "No one is paying attention to us. I'd rather save my energy for now, if it's alright, Captain."

"Just be ready, then."

The order was unnecessary. Solaris had been sitting with is staff across his legs since they saw the first ships. His relaxed hands contrasted sharply with the worried look on his face. With all joking put aside, Rance thought she was glimpsing a look at the real Solaris, the somber, dangerous, Galaxy Wizard one.

"Did Unity abandon Prometheus completely?" Rance

asked, thinking aloud. "It doesn't make sense. Prometheus is a Core world. Triton would never leave it defenseless."

"Unity must have been overwhelmed early on," Solaris said. "But they'll be back. And with more firepower. This place is about to get a whole lot more interesting."

"Captain?" James said. "What do you want to do?"

"If Unity is on the way," Solaris added. "We don't want to be caught here when they arrive. It'll be a bloodbath."

"Captain?"

"I'm thinking, James!"

If they landed on the planet, they had no guarantee of leaving again. Rance's flight suit was starting to feel hot. She tugged on her collar, hoping to allow some airflow to her skin. But the sweat began to bead on her forehead too.

She didn't want to abandon Moira. What if she were still stuck down there, alone and scared? What if Rance and the *Star Streaker* were her only way out?

"Right now, everything looks peaceful," she said, ignoring the fear rising in her throat. She'd made her decision. "We don't need much time."

At that moment, one of the tiny ships in the center of the field exploded in a blinding flash of white light. All the other tiny ships scattered like leaves in the wind.

The Renegades had begun firing.

"Get out!" Rance said.

James swooped beneath another space cruiser, rolling to the side to avoid hitting its short stubby wing. As they passed, another blinding flash of light told them a nearby ship had exploded—a large civilian transport. Then, one by one, ship after ship transformed into bursts of light. Smaller fighters dodged around the bigger ships, taking out the cruisers that tried to run. It looked like a fireworks display, set against the backdrop of sparkling Prometheus. It was as if the pirates had thrown a horrific, planet-wide party.

The display sickened Rance, but she couldn't stop watching in horror as ship after ship exploded into millions of pieces.

"Sons of Triton!" James said. "They're going to kill them all!"

"Us too." Rance leaned forward, watching the screens for signs of anyone locking onto the *Streaker*.

Solaris stood, extending his staff until it was almost as tall as he. Then he raised it over his head, knocking the ceiling as he did so.

He brought it down on the floor with a crack.

Bright white light filled the cockpit. At first, Rance thought one of the Renegades had finally hit the *Star Streaker*. Then she realized Solaris was doing something to the ship. It quivered and shuddered, and James sprang back from his controls.

"What are you doing? He's taken over the ship!"

Rance didn't even know he could do that.

Warning, Deliverance said. *I've lost control of all systems, Captain.*

How was Deliverance still working?

Rance didn't have time to contemplate the seriousness of that before the gravity control went crazy, pulling her away from her chair one minute, tossing her to the side the next. She gripped her armrests as hard as she could and prayed this was all part of Solaris' plan. Amazingly, Solaris remained standing as if his feet were glued to the floor.

Rance couldn't believe it, but she didn't have time to

watch him as the ship pitched forward. She pitched with it, thanking the Founders she was strapped in. Then the gravity shifted to the ceiling, and all the blood rushed to her head.

Warning. Warning. The red words flashed across her vision. She didn't need that added reminder of their danger, so she closed her eyes. But the ZOD played anyway, and the red *Warning* signal against the back of her eyelid only made her more fearful. She opened her eyes again.

Outside, the surrounding ships exploded in more fiery bursts of light. One of them was so close that stars ghosted across Rance's vision.

Bile rose in her throat. The extreme motion felt like she'd been thrown into a box and was being shaken around. Her harness jangled at every turn but held.

Rance kept her mouth shut to prevent herself from biting her tongue, and to keep from vomiting all over James.

Don't puke, don't puke, don't puke.

Whatever Solaris did was working. Although ships around them exploded, the *Star Streaker* remained safe. Rance wanted to ask him what he was doing, but she didn't dare interrupt his concentration now. Or open her mouth—in case something unexpected flew out.

After a few more heart-stopping moments, the *Streaker* charged for Prometheus. Now, Rance finally saw the beautiful green parks and bright seas that covered the planet.

As soon as the ship entered Prometheus' atmosphere, Solaris collapsed onto the floor. The *Star Streaker* righted itself. Deliverance took over the ship's equilibrium, and the red warning stopped. Rance breathed a sigh of relief.

Suddenly, the comm chatter that had been suppressed exploded into the cockpit at once. The yelling crew, the last words of the people on the exploding ships, and distress calls from the planet itself. Somehow, whatever Solaris had done had allowed the *Star Streaker* to filter in all these communications.

The sound was overwhelming. Rance put her hands to her ears, trying to keep the pain at bay.

Now that James had the controls, the ship was flying on a direct course for the capital city. No one chased them. The pirates were too busy killing off the other ships behind.

Since the *Streaker* was no longer trying to kill her, Rance unbuckled her harness and jumped out of her seat. She kneeled over Solaris. His face was white and slick with sweat.

"Solaris!" she yelled over all the noise. "Solaris!"

She slapped his face, but he was out cold. Rance returned to her chair and tried to find a way to shut off the radio chatter. She flipped switches, but when none of that worked, she shouted the request to Deliverance to shut off their communication. That finally did the trick. Every bit of noise was suddenly cut off, plunging the ship into sudden silence.

CHAPTER FIVE

PROMETHEUS WAS a city of tall buildings and wide thoroughfares. The lush green vegetation of parks broke up glass and metal buildings that jutted up into the sky. James set the *Star Streaker* down at the edge of a park, near a tall, dark building. When Rance looked up, she expected to see the fireworks display. But all she saw was bright sunlight filtering through the atmosphere.

People were running everywhere—through the park, in the streets. Ships of all sizes flew overhead, ferrying people away from the mass panic, unaware of the massacre going on above. They narrowly avoided colliding with each other in their haste to get out of the city.

There was a riot going on in the park. Rance noted its location so they could avoid it when they left the *Star Streaker*.

"Captain," James said, turning to look directly at her. "I don't want you to go out there. I know you want to find your friend, but what if she already got out on one of those other cruisers?"

"She was afraid, remember?"

"Yes, but a lot could have changed in the six days it took us to get here. It's too dangerous out there, Rance." James rarely used her name—all joking had been put aside. He was serious.

"We're here, James. We can't turn back now." Rance stood from her chair, went back to Solaris, and shook him again. His face was still ashen, his breathing shallow. Whatever he'd done up there to save their lives must have cost him dearly.

"Solaris! Solaris!"

Then Harper's dark, spiky hair appeared out of the hatch in the floor. She climbed into the cockpit and knelt over Solaris.

"He used up all his power, didn't he?" she asked.

"Yes!"

Harper pulled a syringe out of her pocket and jabbed the needle into his upper arm. She injected the entire contents— a clear, sparkling liquid Rance recognized as an adrenaline cocktail.

She held her breath, waiting to see if it had any effect on the CO. The next moment, Solaris sat bolt upright with a gasp, almost knocking Harper back down the ladder. She scrambled away, backing against a control panel. Solaris looked around with wild eyes, his hair sticking up more than usual. When he saw Rance peering at him, he relaxed.

"What happened?" he asked.

"I don't know. You did something up there, saved our lives. And then you passed out."

Solaris touched the back of his head where it had hit the floor. Then he winced. His hand came away with blood. "Have we landed?"

"Yes." Rance was glad he didn't look permanently damaged. She put an arm under his shoulders and pulled. Solaris helped, and when he got his legs under him, he could stand. His face looked pale and blotchy.

"We landed," Rance said, "but we don't have much time. It looks like they're planning an invasion."

Solaris looked out the window at the ships zooming overhead. "I remember now—they were killing everybody," he whispered.

"Do you have any idea why Unity isn't here?"

"No," he said, shaking his head. He winced. "It doesn't make sense that they would abandon an entire planet and leave it for invasion."

James shrugged out of his harness and joined them. "They must have overwhelmed the forces here before they could call for help. And then they jammed all outside communications."

"But this is a busy star center," Harper said. "When other ships arrived, they would have reported it."

"Not if the pirates surprised them with overwhelming force." Solaris shook his head and then winced again.

"Are you going to be okay?" Rance asked.

"I think so," he said.

Harper grabbed his sleeve and pulled him toward the ladder. "Let's look at your head and make sure you don't need me to close that wound," she said. "Captain, I'll have him ready in a few minutes."

Solaris allowed himself to be led downstairs to the med bay.

Rance turned to James.

He scowled at her. "Captain, we joke around a lot. And because of that, maybe you're not taking me seriously. I'm going to be the practical one here, but is this worth it?"

"I don't know, James. But I hope that if I were in the same situation, someone would try to get me out."

"You know we would. But Moira isn't one of us, and you don't know where she is. At least let me try to get us into the right neighborhood. I don't think we're even in the vicinity."

"Not a good idea. With all the ships flying around, the pirates will target those soon. From here all the way to the river, the only good landing places are on the tops of buildings. The *Streaker* will be an easy target. And it'll be hard to set it down in the middle of a street without drawing unnecessary attention to ourselves."

"It's a risk I'm willing to take if it means our total time here is reduced."

"No, James, we're not far. I promise to radio you and tell you when to come get us."

With that, she left the cockpit, sliding down the ladder and hurrying to her quarters. There, she grabbed a small backpack, one that would hold water and a little food if they found some. On the way out, she grabbed the guns she had prepared—a blaster and a rifle—and her helmet.

Rance couldn't explain why she felt so strongly about going to find Moira. Maybe it was because if Rance had chosen a different path in life, she could be the one stuck without help. Or it could be her mother, stranded in a panicked city. Her mother no longer returned to Prometheus, so Rance wasn't worried about her just now. But now that she had seen what was happening on the planet, she couldn't abandon their mission.

In the back of her mind, Rance knew she was being reckless. But they were already here, and Solaris had almost killed himself to land them. If they didn't try to find Moira, Rance would always regret it.

Down in the cargo bay, Solaris was already waiting on her, looking tired but better. He leaned on his staff and had his satchel slung over his shoulder. The staff looked out of place with his flight suit.

"Did you ever wear robes as a Galaxy Wizard?" Rance asked.

"Why would I wear robes?"

"To make you look the part?"

"Robes would only get in the way. I wanted to catch criminals, not give them something to laugh about when I got tangled up in robes and fell on my face."

"I always thought people with robes looked graceful."

"That's because you grew up with people around you who didn't have to fight for a living."

"True."

Abel stood in his dark gray armor at the galley door, armed with two guns—a rifle and smaller blaster, two knives, and enough ammunition to take out a tank. Next to him, Rance felt very under-armed. But it was Solaris she was concerned about.

"Please take another weapon," she said.

He laughed. "Captain, I just used my staff to deflect an entire pirate army's worth of fire. And you don't think I could use it to protect myself—and you?"

"I don't need you to protect me," she said. "But Moira may need a lot of help."

Solaris moved past her, saying as he went by, "I'll protect you if you need it, Captain, whether you want me to or not."

He was so infuriating sometimes.

Tally stood by the door, his green eyes watching her every move. Rance hated that look. It meant he was worried about her. As he pushed the button to lower the ramp, he said, "Come back to us in one piece."

Then the relative quiet of the hold shattered as the chaos from outside pierced the hull.

The wall of noise hit them like a physical punch. Sirens blared throughout the city, shaking windows and trees in a wavering Doppler effect that made Rance dizzy. Her ears began to throb before she even left the *Streaker*.

On another wavelength, the sounds of chaos underpinned everything. People ran past the ship shouting and yelling at each other. More fights had broken out down the street.

Rance looked back at the *Star Streaker*, knowing that the ship would be vulnerable while they were gone. It was ripe for stealing.

She never underestimated the power of panic. If someone decided to get into the ship, they would find a way to do it. James, Tally, and Harper would only be able to protect themselves by taking off, and it wasn't as if they could go into orbit and wait for Rance to get back.

Solaris must have had the same thought because as the

ship closed, he faced it with his staff in front of him. More sweat broke out on his brow, and Rance could tell he still hadn't recovered from his ordeal. Despite his weariness, he managed to camouflage the ship. She gasped as the *Star Streaker* dissolved from their view, blending into the background of the buildings behind it. It wasn't invisible, exactly. But it had changed patterns, like a chameleon.

The only way anyone would find it would be to run straight into it. With all the people running about, that might happen. But Rance was relying on the chaos to keep anyone from becoming too curious even if they did.

The blaring sirens were too much. She pulled on her helmet and tapped the visor down, which helped with some of the noise. Solaris and Abel did the same. Abel had a heads-up display inside his helmet, and Rance's NNR picked up the city networks and immediately projected a map into her vision. Looking around to be sure no one was paying attention, they ran toward an alley.

"Which way, Captain?" Abel asked once they stood inside the alley.

"She'll be in the residential Senate section," Rance said. "That's where we're headed."

"Do you know the way from here?" Solaris asked.

Rance nodded. "It's been a while, but I know where we're going. My father has a house there."

A moment later they were winding their way through back alleys, heading in the direction indicated by Rance's map. Since Rance had never used the back alleys before, they would rely on the maps as much as possible.

On previous visits to the city, she'd always accompanied her father whenever possible. The lush, green vegetation and the clean air were always welcome changes from her home planet of Xanthes. Now though, with the current of fear running into the very foundation of the city, Rance thought Prometheus could have been a different place altogether.

Without the maps, they would have been lost within ten minutes. The back alleys and darkened passageways between buildings proved to be a labyrinth of metal, concrete, and closed doorways. They could have wandered around the alleys for days while the city burned down around them. Even with the maps, the alleys were so convoluted that they soon lost their sense of direction.

They met no one. Rance felt sure others would try to use the alleys. Where was everybody?

After an hour of wandering through the labyrinth, she began to feel suffocated. The buildings stretched up around them on all sides with a sliver of daylight shining down into the crevasse between. But the sun was sinking, and she didn't want to be trapped in the alley at night. They would have an even harder time getting out after dark.

Rance stopped. They had a choice, to either turn around and go back the way they'd come—if they could find their way back out again—or to continue using the maps, which hadn't been very helpful in leading them out.

"This is pointless," she said.

"I don't know about you, Captain," Abel said, "but I think we should either go back the way we came, or let Solaris unlock one of these doors and walk through the buildings out the other side."

"Then we run the risk of getting lost inside the buildings," Rance said. "I vote we keep going."

Abel shrugged. "You're the boss, boss. We follow you."

"Okay then. But if we get stuck in here and wonder around until the pirates come down and get us, I'm holding you both responsible."

"I don't think it's going to matter. The pirates will never find us in here. They'd have to blow the buildings apart."

Solaris looked at Rance and smiled nervously. She hated when he did that like he didn't really know what he was doing. But she knew better. Solaris was smart and quick on his feet. Whatever he was thinking, he was keeping it to himself. That worried her even more. Solaris usually spoke his mind. She wondered what else was bothering him, but she didn't want to see the buildings fall on top of them.

Time to move on.

They walked a few more minutes, taking two more turns and letting the map guide them toward the center of the city.

"Why haven't we met anybody?" Solaris asked.

"Don't know," Rance muttered, unwilling to face the fact that she had made the wrong decision.

They turned two more corners, and then Abel, who had been walking beside Rance, pulled up short. "You hear that, boss?"

"Hear what?"

They all strained to listen. Their breathing echoed loudly in the empty alley.

"I don't hear—" Solaris began.

"Wait!" Rance whispered. "I did hear something."

She unlatched her helmet and took it off. The internal speakers would magnify anything, but she wanted to know if what she was hearing was real or just feedback from something else. An unusual wind blew through the alley, prickling the hairs on the back of her neck.

Then she heard it again, something scraping along the pavement, clacking, rather, in quick succession. It grew louder, and Rance spun on her heel to look behind. Nothing. Then, along with the clacking sound, they heard a snarl come from an alley ahead. The three turned as one toward the sound.

Rance crept toward the alley, screwed up her courage, and peeked around the corner.

A giant, wolf-like animal, with scales and feathers on its legs and mottled gray hair on its back, was running down the alley.

When it saw her, its nostrils flared. It bared its teeth, revealing unusually large, yellow fangs.

At least, Rance thought they were unusually large.

She hid around the corner, desperately trying to get a hold of her common sense. But all she could see were those fangs. The clacking sound continued—the creature's claws on the ground.

It was getting closer.

Abel and Solaris, curious about what was causing Rance's panic, leaned around the corner to look.

"NO!" she said.

A huge snarl erupted from the animal's mouth, mingled with a high-pitched squawk. It sounded like a dog and a bird had mated, and their offspring was now intent on killing the three of them with its voice alone.

"Run!" Solaris said.

Abel and Rance didn't need to be told again. They sprinted down the alley from which they had come, all three of them stealing glances behind. But the beast didn't give chase, and Rance halted them.

"Wait," she said. "Where'd it go?"

Then something hit her so hard she flew sideways into a wall. All her breath was knocked out of her, and she banged her head as she fell to the ground.

Solaris and Abel were yelling, but she couldn't shake the ringing in her ears. If the *Star Streaker* had landed on top of her, she didn't think she could feel any worse. Disoriented and confused, Rance tried to stand, struggling to get a leg beneath her.

The next second, a great snarling sound overtook the ringing, and she managed to open her bleary eyes.

The bird-wolf stood over her. If it hadn't stopped to snarl, she'd already be dead. Solaris and Abel's shouting seemed far away. All she could do was look at the great fangs hovering over her face. At the big splash of drool dripping onto her nose.

She wanted to pull her visor down, a pitiful barrier between her and the beast. But her visor wasn't there. Where was her helmet? Rance vaguely remembered taking it off, but she didn't know where it had landed.

Then everything became a blur again as a great purple shield hit the animal and knocked it sideways into the wall. Solaris had planted himself in the middle of the alley, his staff held out in front of him. Transparent purple waves of energy emanated from him, creating a barrier between her and the creature. It shrieked and fought back, trying to burst through the shield.

Rance scrambled to get up as the animal tried to recover from Solaris' onslaught. Her head ached, and she felt blood trickling down the back of her neck. The next minute, Abel had his hands under her armpits and was hauling her to her feet. Every bit of her hurt, but as soon as she was upright, she stood without assistance.

The beast yelped.

Rance and Abel jerked their attentions back to the ongoing battle. Rance expected it to turn and run. Instead, it gathered itself and charged.

In a great leap of power, the creature burst through Solaris' shield.

Solaris was hammered back against the wall while his shield disappeared around him. But the bird-wolf hadn't expected to break through and had already turned for another charge.

As the animal turned to lunge for Solaris, Rance seized her rifle from the ground. She used her ZOD to line up a shot at the beast's head and fired. The rounds bounced off the animal and disappeared.

But the diversion gave Solaris enough time to scramble to his feet. Rance continued to fire as the creature lunged for him, its fangs bared. Solaris pushed his staff out ahead of him, creating the energy shield again, and the animal bounced off. But the blow barely fazed it, and it climbed to his feet, huffing and angry.

Rance fired, again and again, the bolts from the energy rifle causing the air to prickle with electricity. Abel had joined her. Drawn by their fire, the beast turned from Solaris, staring at the tiny humans trying to get its attention. It squawked again.

Without waiting for it to attack again, Rance yelled and charged the creature.

"Rance! No!" Solaris yelled as his shield disappeared.

Abel yelled too, and charged after her.

Sensing a challenge, the bird-wolf pounded the pavement toward Rance. Its fangs opened wide, expecting an easy meal. At the last second, Rance leaned back and skidded onto her back. The animal bellowed at her sudden course change.

Teeth slid past her head, and her momentum sent her sliding between its front legs. Rough concrete grated down her back, tearing her suit. As the creature's belly slid by, Rance fired. She managed to get off three shots before it jumped out of the way.

Abel launched himself into the air and landed on the animal's neck. He tried to grab a handful of fur, but he slid down as it shook its large head. Dangling off the creature's neck, Abel extended a blade from his armor and stabbed. The powerful blow should have torn through the animal's hide, but instead the blade glanced off the fur in a shower of sparks. The bird-wolf howled and shook its head, sending Abel flying down the alley.

Painfully aware of how close the animal now was, Rance scrambled to her feet, firing straight into its hairy back. The animal turned and swiped its long tail over the top of her head. Only then did she see the sharp spike at the end of it. She ducked and rolled to the side to avoid being impaled.

As it sprang for her again, Solaris' shield returned, and this time it encapsulated the whole animal. He stood dangerously close to it, watching its every move and waiting for it to break free. Beads of sweat ran down his face and fogged up his visor.

Behind Solaris, Abel lay on his side, crumpled near a wall. He slowly stood to his feet. Other than being stunned, his suit had protected him. Rance thanked the Founders that he had not been bitten. Solaris must've done something to prevent it.

She went to Solaris' side.

"I couldn't cast the shield around it while you were so close," he accused. His words were clipped as he concentrated on trapping the animal.

"I didn't think about it before I did it."

"That was obvious." Solaris shot her a look, but he didn't look angry.

The creature struggled, beating against the shield. With each blow, the shield looked thinner, as if it were stretching beyond its endurance. Now that she wasn't running or charging it, Rance could take a closer look at the animal. It was only then she realized that the hair on its back was not fur, but spikes. She shuddered, thinking how close she'd come to brushing up against them.

With each blow to the shield, the spikes scraped along it, leaving little tiny sparks. Was the animal magical? Was that why it was able to fight Solaris?

Solaris had said there was no such thing as magic though.

The creature hit the shield one more time, and a great tearing sound echoed throughout the alley. Rance held up her gun, prepared to shoot. But she didn't know what good it would do.

The shield was still in place, but the tear grew wider and wider at each successive blow. Solaris struggled to keep it together.

Rance nodded to Abel, and they both trained their weapons on the animal. She noticed blood dripping from its belly where she had shot it. That's where it was vulnerable.

But when the shield broke, how would they manage to shoot its belly before it killed them?

Then she had an idea. A really stupid, crazy idea.

"Solaris!" Rance yelled. The tearing sound grew, and the creature roared, blocking out her voice. When Solaris glanced at her, she said, "Roll it over!"

Just then, the shield broke, and the resulting shockwave rolled through the alley and hit the three of them, sending them backward like a small bomb had detonated. Rance went head over heels into the pavement. Terrified that those fangs would sink into her flesh while she lay there, Rance ignored the new pain in her body and pushed herself to her feet.

Solaris had regained his footing first, and as the animal turned to him, he hit it with a different type of shield.

Instead of creating a bubble, it created a wall, blocking off the alley and pushing the animal away from them. The creature fell on its side, shrieking. Fearing her eardrums would burst, Rance covered her ears. But Solaris had something else in mind.

"On the count of three!" he yelled.

Rance grabbed her rifle and trained it on the beast. Beside her, Abel followed suit.

"One, two, three!"

Solaris released the wall, and Rance and Abel fired their weapons on the animal's underbelly, over and over until the air was thick with smoke and the burned smell of their weapons. Rance ran out of ammo long before Abel, who reloaded several times. She grabbed her pistol, ready to keep going.

They still weren't doing enough damage. Despite the firepower being directed at it, the animal scrambled to its feet and jumped up out of the way. Rance saw a flash of teeth and aimed for it. Her rounds bounced off its fangs in sparks that lit the alleyway, lighting up the smoke like lightning in a storm.

Then, a tooth exploded. The creature shook its head and halted, a look of confusion in its eyes. Just as Rance was about to fire again, it ducked its head and whimpered.

"That's interesting," Rance muttered.

Abel paused to reload. "What do we do, boss?"

"I have no idea."

"Maybe it just wanted to play with us, and you hurt its feelings," Solaris said. He was breathing heavily and looked almost as weak as he had when he'd collapsed in the cockpit.

"Play with its food, you mean."

"At least we know why no one was using the alleys," Abel said. "I wonder how long this thing's been living out here?"

The animal was blocking their escape. Running back through the alleys would only give the creature a bigger advantage. It probably knew every shortcut. If they turned and ran, it would no doubt burst out in front of them again.

And then Rance had another idea. The creature shook its head. Spittle and blood went flying, coating the alley walls. Again, it focused on its tiny prey, looking ready to fight again. Rance holstered her weapon and raised her arms, waving them around wildly.

"Hey!" she yelled. "Over here you stupid animal!"

"Uh, Captain?" Solaris asked.

"What are the chances of getting it to chase us?" Rance asked.

"I thought that's what it was doing," Solaris said, rolling his eyes. "If that's not chasing us, I don't know what is."

"Okay," she said. "Your shield can't stop it, and our weapons can't hurt it. So, we have to do something else."

"My shield is just fine!"

"You can disguise the ship, manipulate gravity, and change your face at will, but you can't generate a shield strong enough to keep this monster away from us!"

The creature wasn't going to give them a chance to stand around arguing about it anymore. After another moment of contemplation, it seemed to have decided Rance was the main threat and fixed an eye on her. A warning message flashed through her vision.

Hostile proximity too close for maneuvering. Suggest running.

Oh great, Rance thought. Even her ZOD was a coward.

"All right, guys," she said, "this is your chance to prove your loyalty to me."

"I hope you're not thinking of doing anything stupid," Solaris said. He kept his eyes on the creature and crouched low, his staff pointing forward like a rifle.

"You haven't known me very long, have you?" Rance said. She took her eyes off the monster for only a moment, to give Solaris her best smile.

The creature charged, running straight for Rance. She turned and sprinted away, yelling over her shoulder, "Trip it!"

She hoped beyond hope that they'd understood her command. Because if they didn't, this creature was going to catch her and eat her.

Then she heard a great roar. A thud shook the alley. Feeling a strange movement of air behind her, she pressed herself to the wall just in time for the creature to fly past her, head over heels. The beast somersaulted until it crashed into a wall at the end of the alley, going straight through and creating a rumble of noise inside one of the buildings.

Rance stepped out and looked at Solaris and Abel.

Solaris looked at his staff, which he'd flung out in front of the charging animal. "It seems like the staff is good for something, at least."

Abel shook his head. "Why didn't your magic stop it?"

"Some creatures are immune to it," Solaris said. "But that doesn't mean that I can't physically trip them. And I added a little extra power so it would be rigid enough to withstand the charge."

He turned to Rance and frowned. "Next time, Captain, would you tell us your plan before you run away?"

"What would be the fun in that?"

"Oh, you know, the adrenaline rush is fun. But I think I'd rather get out with my captain in one piece than go on a thrill-seeking mission."

Rance's grin faded. Solaris had a way of taking the fun right out of the adventure. Still, she *had* been worried there for a minute. So maybe his concern wasn't unfounded. She shrugged it off and went to find her helmet.

It lay down another alley, having been cast aside when she was first attacked. She wished she'd been wearing it when the monster had knocked her over. Her head throbbed painfully. She was only just noticing it.

Before leaving, the three stood watching the hole in the wall. Inside, the creature was still thrashing around, squawk-roaring.

"Do you think there are any people in there?" Rance asked.

"We would have heard the screams by now, I think," Solaris said.

"Boss, let's get out of here before it finds its way out of that hole."

Solaris tried to look at the wound on Rance's head, but she mashed on her helmet and strode off down the alley, ready to resume following the map. Wavy lines crossed her vision, and the grid faded from view. The blow to her head must have interrupted the signal between her NNR and ZOD.

Rance tapped the back of her helmet to jar it. The action sent shooting pain up into her brain. She jerked her hand away. They would have to follow Abel's map from here.

During the fight, they had got twisted around. Abel led them through turn after turn, each alley looking exactly like the one before it. Just as Rance was beginning to think they'd wander the in-between spaces of the city forever, everything became familiar.

"Haven't we been here before?" Solaris asked.

"Yes," Rance said. "I think so."

"The map says we are almost out to the street," Abel said.

Finally, Rance recognized a series of doorways she thought they had passed on their way in. She jogged over, peeking around the corner of the building. There, just down from where she was standing, was the street they'd used to enter.

She growled in frustration and motioned for the others to follow. The *Star Streaker* was hidden up the street. Rance looked at Solaris, who confirmed that it was still there, invisible and safe. The comm crackled with James' voice, sending more throbbing pain through her already sensitive head.

"What in the Founders' name are you doing, Rance Cooper?"

"I thought we'd take the scenic tour of the city, James."

"I don't know if you've noticed, Captain, but we're seeing fewer civilian ships and more fighting. Be careful, please."

"Why James, it's like you're worried about me."

"This isn't funny, Captain."

"I'm not laughing. Save the gooey stuff until I get back to the *Star Streaker* though, huh?"

James clicked off, and Rance thought she'd probably offended him. No, their situation wasn't funny at all. Sometimes, she didn't know how to behave when people expressed concern for her. Even those who loved her. But she didn't have time for his sentimentality. They'd lost a lot of time, and if they didn't find a way through the city soon, they'd be stuck without shelter at nightfall. Also, she had no idea when the pirates would begin landing.

"You know," Solaris said as they jogged along. "Every time I've been to Prometheus, I've always wondered why the city refused to have a stronger military presence. It's a Core world, and with all the nobility and officials living here, you'd think that they would demand a stronger show of force."

"It's because they were always a Core world that they didn't bother with it," Rance said. "My father always complained that they were too confident for their own good. Looks like he was right about this, at least."

The Core worlds, buffered by endless colonies in between them and alien planets, had grown soft. They had become complacent in their own power. Prometheus was no better. Although it held the financial seat of the empire, and a secondary parliament for the Outer Colonies, it behaved as if it were Triton itself—strong and invincible and arrogant.

Although the pirates had been gaining numbers in recent years, no one ever thought they would join to become anything more than ragged, scrabbling individual clans.

"Why didn't your father do anything about it?" Solaris asked. "I thought he had some influence."

"He has *some* influence. He has influence on his own planet, less in the Senate. He doesn't have enough clout to determine how much military the Core worlds keep around."

Abel moved ahead, checking around the corner of the building for any obstacles before motioning to Rance and Solaris. Then he said, "They were so busy worried about the aliens out beyond the Outer Colonies, they forgot to protect themselves against their own kind."

"You're right, Abel," Solaris said. "Sometimes we humans forget we're capable of just as much damage as any outsiders."

"As much as I love your need to discuss philosophy," Rance said, "I'd rather focus on our immediate surroundings and the gang of thugs that just walked out that alleyway up ahead."

Four large men watched them from the street, lazily though, like they weren't too interested. They didn't look like pirates—that is, they weren't covered in tattoos and didn't carry large weapons. But they didn't exactly look friendly. One of them caught Rance looking and shifted direction for them.

That was enough for Rance.

"Let's go around them," she said. "Follow me."

She crossed the street, stepping left around a large transport abandoned near a building. Except for Abel's weapons and armor, they didn't have much for anybody to steal. But she didn't want to take any chances. She broke into a run, going until she had a stitch in her side and they had put some distance between themselves and the thugs. The jogging made her head pound with every step.

"I think we lost them," Solaris said. "You still know where we are?"

"Yes. I think so."

She hoped so. They rounded a corner.

And ran straight into an angry mob.

CHAPTER SIX

A CROWD HAD GATHERED in the street. Sounds of shouting and breaking glass bounced off the towers and echoed back to them. Thick, sharp-smelling smoke drifted down the street. The crowd had concentrated around a tall tower which was on fire.

"Are they mad?" Solaris asked.

"The fire won't get far," Rance said. "The building's protective systems will kick in before it does much damage."

Solaris shook his head. "I'm not talking about the fire."

Rance and Abel looked to where he nodded. Just outside the crowd, a man, woman, and two children were loading a small transport with bags. The youngest, a boy of about six, was carrying a bag twice his size.

A group of men noticed the family and broke off from the main crowd. The father saw them and threw the remaining bags into the back. The woman and girl climbed in, and he had just put the little boy into the cruiser when one of the men grabbed him by the tunic. He hurled him away from the transport while the other thugs swarmed the vehicle. Inside, the girl cried, and the woman pleaded with them.

Solaris grumbled and shrugged off his satchel, letting it fall to the ground.

"Wait a minute, Solaris," Rance said. "Where are they going to go in the transport?"

He scowled. "It's none of my business. Are you suggesting we don't do anything?"

"I didn't say that."

Just then, one of the thugs grabbed the boy and tossed him out of the vehicle too. The father yelled something and caught the boy before he hit the ground. Rance grew hot with anger. As much as she didn't want to get sidetracked from their goal, she couldn't stand by and do nothing.

The little drive on the transport spun up. The thugs were going to take off with the woman and daughter inside.

Without a word, Rance, Solaris, and Abel sprang into action, running to reach the transport before it took off. They skidded to a halt at the door. Solaris stuck his staff in, holding it open. Then he reached into the pilot's side and landed a quick jab to the man's throat.

The man choked, spitting and going red in the face. In the meantime, Rance grabbed the little girl out of her seat while Abel tackled the second man inside the transport.

Before Rance could pull the little girl out of the cruiser, hands grabbed at her back and then latched onto her helmet. Whoever had a hold of her was trying to pull her out of the transport by her head. With a pop, the latch sealing her helmet to her suit broke apart. Rance yelled and spun around, trying to use her elbow to whack her attacker.

It was the girl's father. Apparently, he thought Rance was trying to attack the girl too.

By now, Abel and Solaris were in an all-out brawl with the other men, who were proving to be stronger than they had seemed. Solaris' staff had disappeared, and he was trading blows with a man who was shorter and stockier than himself. Abel had a second man in a headlock while a third threw himself onto his shoulders with gusto. Warming to the fight, Abel flung both men away. When they rose, he turned to face them, a smile on his face.

"Oh, for Triton's sake," Rance said, still grappling with the little girl's father. "Stop being gentlemen and knock them out!"

Solaris must have heard her because he found his staff again and used it. After a few tense seconds, he knocked out two men while Abel ran off the third.

The father still held onto Rance's helmet, but somehow it had hung up on the broken latch and wouldn't come off. Being led around by the head was making her angry. She grabbed the man's hands to steady herself and aimed an awkward kick at his knees. He howled in pain but refused to let go.

Abel returned, saw the father attacking Rance, and ran toward them. The man, seeing a large hulking form running straight at him, let go of Rance. His wife joined him, and they took off down the street with their children.

Rance took a deep, steadying breath. Her neck hurt where he'd jerked her around, but other than that she wasn't injured any more than she had been before. Solaris and Abel seemed okay as well. The three turned to leave when one of the thugs climbed to his feet and got into the transport.

"He's leaving his buddies behind," Solaris said.

"Did you expect any different?" Rance asked. "There's no honor among people like that."

They watched the little transport shoot straight up into the air, following the line of the tall buildings. Rance craned her neck to watch it make for the gap between two skyscrapers.

At the same moment, a large cruiser careened out of the gap, a gaping hole in its side. The little transport flew straight into one of the cruiser's engines and exploded into a fireball. The cruiser's engine caught fire as well, and the entire ship veered toward the burning building.

When it collided with the tower, the ground shook like an earthquake, the impact rattling Rance's bones. Instead of bouncing off or smashing through, it slid down with a horrendous screech, raining glass and fire on the crowd below. People ran screaming as the fireball grew toward them.

The tangled ships hit the ground with the force of a bomb exploding. The glass in neighboring buildings shattered, and Rance covered her head as shards fell on her. An explosion followed, and a great wall of fire swept over the buildings. It barreled down the street, devouring everything in its path.

Too fast for Rance and crew to escape.

Her ZOD chose that moment to begin working.

Danger. Danger. Danger.

Rance stared as the deadly flames swept toward them. Too shocked even to feel scared, she waited for her death. She thought about her mother, Davos, even Solaris standing beside her. At the last second, unable to face the fire that would consume her, she ducked.

She waited, cringing. Expecting to feel a shock of pain

before it was all over. It would disintegrate her to the bone, but at least it would be quick.

But Rance felt nothing.

She looked up, wondering why she wasn't dead yet. And saw Solaris, standing over her and Abel with his staff in hand, that transparent bubble returned, shielding them from the blast. He looked for all the world as if he were a statue placed there to protect them from harm.

When the worst passed in a wave of fire and smoke, he released the shield.

Rance and Abel stood, slowly removing their arms from over their heads and gaping at Solaris.

He smiled and winked at Rance. "I didn't think *you* needed saving, Captain, but you know, Abel looked like he could use some help."

Rance stared at him open-mouthed. If she'd thought he was talented before, she was in awe of him now. His power, with the ship, with the fire, was unbelievable. Solaris gazed at her intently.

Never one to be overwhelmed by feelings, Abel clapped Solaris on the back in thanks as he moved past him. The force, amplified by Abel's powered armor, sent Solaris reeling forward. He regained his balance and looked at the fire consuming the other buildings.

"They're going to go, too," he said. "We better get moving."

The trio turned down a side street and jogged all the way to the end. Smoke blew toward them, bringing the acrid smell of burning fuel and metal along with it.

When they entered the next street, Rance knew exactly where they were. To see better, she turned off her malfunctioning ZOD and led them by memory, watching for any more riots or crazed thugs. A turn, then down another street framed by twisty trees. Rance had forgotten what they were called, but then she'd never been very good with plants. Xanthes didn't have many.

Putting aside the tragedy several streets over, Rance was proud they had gotten this far. At this rate, they'd find Moira and get back to the *Star Streaker* before nightfall. When they came out the end of the street, though, Rance realized she'd forgotten one very important thing.

In front of them, a wide, fast-flowing river obstructed their way forward. To their right, a gigantic bridge spanned across the water.

Or it would have if the middle hadn't been blown out. A large Unity police ship had crashed into the river, taking out the bridge with it. With the river in front, and the growing fire behind, they were trapped.

"Somehow, I don't think the river is going to be our worst problem," Solaris said.

"There's got to be another bridge," Abel said.

"Far, far down at the other end of the city," Rance said.

Most of the citizens used air transport, so the bridge was mainly for foot traffic. It was used for parades and official transportation only. Rance sighed. What were they going to do now?

"Any bright ideas, Captain?" Solaris said. He leaned out over the edge of the water, looking down into the churning current. The water had a metallic smell Rance remembered. Tally had once told her it was because of the water treatments it underwent as it was recycled back into the river from the underground drains.

He'd also told her about the vast underground tunnels beneath the city. Rance cringed as she remembered.

Not underground.

She looked around, desperately wishing for another idea to present itself. But the smoke behind obscured the view of the sky. Fewer ships were flying about now. Either they'd all been shot down or had met with accidents like the one they'd just witnessed.

Abel coughed. With the smoke growing thicker by the minute, they couldn't stay where they were. And they couldn't cross the river.

They didn't have a choice.

With a deep sigh, Rance turned to Solaris and Abel. "We can't go over the river, but we can go under."

Surprisingly, they didn't have any trouble finding an entrance down. In fact, doors were available at regular intervals throughout the city.

"Why do they make them so easy to find?" Abel asked as they went down a well-lit, wide staircase beyond a door in the nearest building.

"Nobles use them to travel unseen within the city. Politicians like ways to move around without being seen." Rance shuddered as they descended the stairs. The first corridor wasn't bad—well-lit, airy, and clean. They met a few people running past them who must have had the same idea.

They followed the corridor, sometimes stepping into a side hallway to avoid running into more people. As they went, the tunnels turned darker. And they weren't well-maintained. Dirt and grime covered the floor and splashed up onto the walls. What lights were available, instead of warm yellow, became white and uninviting.

Doors were everywhere. Occasionally they passed one that had the hum of a machine behind it. The smell of warm grease pervaded everything, mixing with the damp air until it stung their eyes and throats. Although dry air was being pumped through, it couldn't eliminate the sticky, cool air of neglect.

The worst part by far was the feeling of being slowly, excruciatingly crushed by the ground above. Rance was okay on a cramped spaceship, but underground was a whole other complication. Her stomach rolled into a knot that wouldn't untie, and she had difficulty breathing. When she did, the smell of grease and foul air almost drove her to turn around and run out. She put her visor down.

Abel led the way. "We have similar tunnels on Triton," he said. "But there, only maintenance and security workers use them."

Abel followed dark, exposed piping above their heads. The ceilings became so low Rance and Solaris had to duck. Despite the cool air, Rance broke out in a sweat. Her clothes became uncomfortable, sticking to her body and making her feel generally gross.

Once, Rance had gone into the mines on Xanthes with her father and Tally. She'd lasted ten minutes before her heart raced and her head began spinning. She almost passed out. Tally had had to escort her out of the mine, to the great displeasure of Davos.

As the tunnel sloped downward, Rance breathed carefully through her nose to keep from panicking. But she didn't say anything. No point in worrying Abel or Solaris.

But when the floor leveled out again and water beaded on the walls, the knot in her stomach turned into a rock.

They were under the river.

"You okay?" Solaris asked.

"Yes," she replied tersely. "Just hurry, okay?"

They picked up the pace, weaving through tunnels that became increasingly darker. Rance worried she would lose her mind, imagined sitting down on the concrete floor, putting her head between her knees, and crying like a baby. But just as she was about to act out her fantasy, the floor began to slope upward.

"You know, boss," Abel said. "I always thought Prometheus was a rich planet. But after seeing these maintenance tunnels, they must have fallen on hard times. No wonder Unity isn't here to defend them."

"Most cities are like this beneath," Solaris said. "The empire isn't as grand as it would seem on the surface."

Rance didn't have any opinions to offer on the matter. Well, she did, but she was too busy trying not to panic or lose her sanity to discuss the state of the empire. Although she was on the run from a barbaric marriage decree, Rance still considered herself a citizen. She cared about the empire, and the cities' dilapidation concerned her.

Beneath her helmet, Rance's hair was soaked with sweat. She forced the broken latch apart to take it off. The smell of grease and dirt was preferable to suffocating inside her own personal sauna.

Finally, the way widened, and they began climbing a hill. They passed intersecting tunnels. Each one became more elaborate, more comfortable than the one before it. They were almost there.

"Where do you think this comes out?" Abel asked.

"Most of these tunnels come up in the residential district," Rance said. "Like I said, the nobles use them quite frequently, although I don't think they travel the one that we just used—it was too dirty."

She breathed more easily now, and her heart rate had slowed to the point where she could deal with it. Maybe she would get out of this alive—and without hyperventilating.

They walked another hour. Gradually, fresh, circulating air dried Rance's hair. The water on the walls dried. And then the corridor ended in a wide staircase leading upwards to the street.

CHAPTER SEVEN

When they exited through a door leading out of the basement of a low, flat building, the first things they noticed were the sirens blaring and the darkness falling. Rance put on her helmet again—gently—and closed the visor. The wind picked up, blowing the smoke away. Just like from the other side of the river, the residential section stretched out as far as the eye could see. Tall, shining buildings, wide parks, and fountains stretched in every direction. The buildings here were farther apart, allowing the green-tinged sunset to light the deserted streets.

Now that the sun had faded, the day was turning cold. Rance shivered. She was weary, hungry, and the weight of her responsibility slowed her down like she was carrying the *Star Streaker* on her back. What if they couldn't get out? What if she couldn't find Moira?

Behind them, on the other side of the river, the fire had spread to other buildings. That way was completely closed off. If they ever found Moira, they'd have to find an alternate route.

Rance had no intention of going back underground. She tried to contact James, who was planning to pick them up. But all she got was static.

For the first time, she doubted whether she could keep her friends safe. She wanted to keep her word even though she hadn't actually spoken with Moira. But she also wanted to keep Solaris and Abel in one piece. It was up to her to protect the crew. She was the captain. And they were her family.

She trudged along, leading them into the darkened section of the city. Rance knew exactly where she was now and headed for Moira's neighborhood. Davos had his own residence in this area, but she was certain her father was nowhere near the planet. At least, she hoped he hadn't been near it, or on one of those ships that had exploded in the barricade.

Rance may have still felt the sting of her father's betrayal, but she didn't wish him dead.

The tall buildings lining the street exuded wealth and power. Once upon a time, Rance would have enjoyed strolling through the streets dressed in fine clothes, her face studded with jewels. But she had not been able to do so for some time, and now that she knew how other people lived, she preferred the life of a free commoner to the life of a pampered noblewoman.

Rance hadn't wanted to admit all this to Solaris when he'd questioned her. But she was embarrassed by who she used to be. She knew she couldn't help where she'd come from, but when she thought of all the silly parties and ridiculous expectations she'd had, she grew angry with herself.

Her anger made her even more determined to get Moira off the planet. It seemed like all the pirates in the galaxy had gathered in this one spot. What were they doing?

Of course, Prometheus was an important planet. It controlled vast swaths of the sector as well as held an important governmental seat on Triton. But without the citizens, the planet wasn't as useful. So, what did the pirates have in mind? Were they simply here to pillage and plunder?

If they were, Rance wouldn't be surprised. She'd grown up hearing terrible stories about the pirates who flew across the galaxy with abandon, perpetrating horrific crimes upon the innocent they encountered.

With a shudder, Rance decided she didn't want to be anywhere near the city when they landed. Which meant they had very little time to get out.

"Where will she be?" Solaris asked.

Rance sent a quick message over her comm, broadcasting again in case Moira was listening. But all she heard was static. "Communications are still down."

"And they'll continue to be until the pirates land," Solaris said. His face turned red, and Rance was about to ask him why when they encountered a group of men walking up the street. Wishing to avoid another confrontation, Rance, Solaris, and Abel moved into the long shadows cast by the buildings.

The men walked on. Rance had the feeling that it was only a matter of time before they would have to fight their way through a crowd. Right now, people were just trying to stay indoors and away from the sirens.

Rance turned to look at Solaris. He was glaring at the men as they walked away. She'd never really seen him angry. "Everything all right?"

"I just wish we had some direction, that's all. For some indication that your friend is even here on this planet where we are wandering around exposed for all to see."

A surge of anger welled up in Rance. "If you didn't want to come, you shouldn't have."

"It's not that," Solaris said, shaking his head. "I don't like pirates."

"Only pirates like pirates," Abel said sagely. "And most of them don't like each other, either."

"Didn't you fight pirates as a Galaxy Wizard?" Rance asked.

"Yes, many and often. Since I was a child, I vowed that any I encountered would feel the full wrath of the Wizards."

Rance frowned. She'd never heard Solaris talk that way. He was usually mild-mannered, and except for the few times he'd been forced to act, it was easy for her to forget that he'd fought in Unity's elite special force.

Rance's comm crackled in her ear, sending an eardrum-splitting squeak into her head. "Ow! Who's doing that?"

"Not me, boss," Abel said, wincing.

"Nor me," Solaris said. He turned on his heel and scanned the dark towers around them. When nothing else came through, they continued their hunt.

Rance decided to make her way to her father's old residence. Moira had lived close by a few years ago. They were taking a chance that she still did, but options were scarce given the circumstances.

They walked for another hour. The planet grew darker,

the deep shadows of night replacing the long shadows of the buildings. Prometheus didn't have a moon, and the stars were blocked by smoke spreading over the city.

They hid from a few more roaming bands, unwilling to find out if they were friend or foe. Every few minutes, Rance tried hailing Moira on an open channel.

As the night went on, the group became even more tired. Rance forced one foot in front of the other, shook her head to keep her eyes open. With no food and no sleep, she was running on pure adrenaline. And even that was failing her.

With his armor to support his weapons as well as his body, Abel didn't complain. Solaris stewed about something. Rance didn't ask what. At that moment, all she could think about was sitting down, putting her head on her knees, and sleeping.

After midnight, the first of Kaur's dark ships flew overhead. The trio ducked into an alley, watching the sky for more. Three more ships passed by before they felt safe enough to move on.

"They're landing, aren't they?" Rance asked.

"Looks like it," Solaris said.

"Will the *Star Streaker* be safe?"

"If James doesn't move it."

"Did you tell him that?"

"No, but where's he going to go?"

"You don't know what he'll be forced to do!"

"True," was all he said. And he refused to argue further.

Rance, fuming, hungry, and cold, was ready to give up. She wanted to, oh so badly. Suddenly, the mission seemed like a foolish errand—an immature, brainless, impulsive errand. Rance mentally kicked herself. If they got off the planet alive, it would be a miracle. She looked at Solaris again, hoping he had at least one more miracle left in him.

Finally, she pulled up her handset to check the status of the *Star Streaker*, but it wouldn't tell her anything, either. She tried to hail James on the comm. All she earned was more squawking in her earpiece.

"You ready to give up, boss?" Abel asked.

"No. I just wanted to check in with them. But it would be great if they could pick us up."

Solaris gave her a sideways glance. "There's no shame in going back, Captain Cooper. To come this far for someone you barely know—it's commendable."

Maybe he was right. She looked into Solaris' blue eyes, wondering what he was really thinking.

He seemed to be thinking one thing and saying something different.

"Do *you* think we should go back?" she asked. She waited for him to respond, but she knew her decision. They'd come this far. If she left now, she'd always regret it. It felt too much like running away.

But you're very good at running away, Devri. She pushed aside the small voice inside her head, the one that liked to remind her of her failings. No use dwelling on the past now. And this situation was different. Moira's life could be in danger. Running away from her father only endangered herself and, to some extent, Tally. Running away from Moira could mean her death.

Solaris, who had been thoughtfully watching the street, finally shook his head. "We're here, might as well assist if we can. If you're right and she was afraid to leave the planet, she's in hiding. I just wish we could get past those jammers."

"Me, too."

Rance tried one more time to raise James or Moira. But when her earpiece sent ringing vibrations into her skull, she stopped trying. Then she looked up at the dark sky with its smoke and glanced around at the quiet buildings. She was just about to suggest they find a place to rest a few minutes when a woman exited the building across the street.

She was dressed in a long robe, the kind that trailed the pavement when she walked. Even from the silhouette, Rance recognized that type. It was a noblewoman's clothing, never meant to touch the ground outside. Only the very wealthy wore robes like that because they never had to walk outside for themselves if they didn't want to. They only wore those fine clothes indoors.

The woman looked both ways up and down the street. Rance didn't try to hide. But when the woman saw them, she shrank back into the shadows of the building.

Rance's comm squawked again. Only this time, a woman's voice was mingled in with the static. It wasn't coming through the earpiece but from across the street.

"Stay here," she told Solaris and Abel. Then she darted across the street, keeping her eye on a band of men three buildings down. The woman saw Rance and turned to go inside.

"Moira?"

The woman stopped, looking Rance up and down as if she didn't believe what she was seeing. Then she approached cautiously, trying to identify Rance in the dark. "Devri? Is it really you? I didn't think I'd reached you."

Rance kept her eyes on the gang of men. They looked like they were checking alleys, checking doors. She didn't like the way they systematically looked at everything. Since it was dark, she couldn't tell if they were pirates or citizens, but this late at night she didn't want to take a chance on either of them.

"I didn't think I'd find you either," Rance said. "Hi, Moira."

Moira grabbed her in a tight hug. The young woman was much shorter than Rance, but her grip was strong. She trembled a bit, and Rance could only imagine how frightened she must have been.

As soon as Solaris and Abel reached them, Moira let go and punched in the code to let them inside.

Inside was dark, but their feet echoed off fine stone. Even the air felt richer.

"This building still has power," Moira said. "But I've kept off the lights to avoid any attention."

"You're the only one left in the building?"

"Just my serving girls are with me—Tania and Sonya."

She led them to an elevator which Rance was happy to see still worked. They stepped onto it, and less than a minute later, it opened on beautiful, expansive living quarters at the top of the building. Plush furniture and AI-controlled amenities covered the entire room. Expansive windows gave them views of the city on four sides, with private rooms in the middle of the building.

From their vantage point, the fires around the city burned like torches at a ceremony—giant torches ringing them in, offering no way out. Warships flew overhead and around, all marked with Pirate Kaur's symbol.

"Moira," Rance said. "I want you to meet some of my crew—Roote and Abel."

"Pleased to meet you," Moira said, offering each of them her hand. "I would offer a party in your honor, but things have changed a little bit around here."

Abel and Solaris both bowed.

"Are you ready to leave?" Solaris asked.

Moira looked confused. "Now?"

"That's why we're here," Rance said. "You asked for help getting off the planet."

"Yes. I did." Moira looked disorientated and stared around the room as if she couldn't think of what to say next.

"Pack one bag, keep it light," Rance said. "We're going to have to find another way back to the *Star Streaker*."

"Is that the name of your ship?"

"Yes."

"And you want to leave now?"

In truth, Rance wanted nothing more than to lay down on one of the cushions in the middle of the room and go to sleep. Her head hurt, her body hurt, even her teeth hurt. Her exhaustion must have shown because Moira suddenly had a look of pity on her face.

"Have you eaten?"

In answer, Abel's stomach rumbled. Solaris walked around the windows, looking out at the city below and the glow of the fires.

Rance sighed. Despite the fact they needed to get out as quickly as possible, she was too tired to think straight. And she was just as hungry as Abel.

"We'll give you some time to pack," she said. "In the meantime, we could use some sleep. And food. Alright with you?"

Moira nodded. "I won't need much time. But you're welcome to sleep anywhere you find a space. There are plenty of rooms. Mine is the first door on the right. Take any other one you choose."

Abel was the first to take her invitation, stomping off to find a door. He disappeared into it right away, and Rance heard his weapons and armor clatter to the floor. Within seconds, his deep snores rang out throughout the house.

Moira clapped her hands, and two young women came out of the shadows.

A feeling of disgust shot through Rance. She'd forgotten how the nobility lived—without a care for those under them. But the girls appeared healthy and well-treated. Both with the same olive skin and dark hair, close in age. Obviously sisters. They skirted around Solaris, who seemed to make them nervous.

Rance thought about that little boy in the marketplace on Ares who had stolen the vagrappes. He was stealing food just to get by, living off scraps and in constant danger of being arrested. Moira, on the other hand, lived a life of ease and didn't even realize it. Rance didn't have anything against people being rich, but it annoyed her that she had felt this way one time herself. Had she ever been like Moira?

"What happened to your husband, Moira?" she asked as the Tania and Sonya fussed over Rance's head injury.

Moira shook her head. "I don't know exactly. He'd been going to secret meetings, at night. He invited a few strange people here once, and they shut themselves up in his office all day. Richard has always been a man of few words, but he's never kept anything from me. At least, he'd always provided me with straight answers if I asked about things."

"He had other things?"

"Mostly I never asked. I have my own responsibilities. But he never hesitated when I did. Except for those new meetings. He'd brush me off. And then our friends began to treat us—me—differently. They shut me out of several parties, but more disturbingly, they refused to do any business with my husband or me. And I still haven't been able to figure out why."

Rance winced as Sonya dabbed a particularly tender spot on her scalp. "So he's involved in some secret society that everyone knows about except you? Ow!"

"Sorry, your Ladyship," Sonya said. "The bleeding has stopped. I'm going to scan your head for a concussion and then we'll patch you up."

Moira shot Rance a reproachful look. "Don't mock me, Devri. I know it is unusual, nor does it make any sense, but I didn't know what to do—"

She broke off in a sob. Moira looked so sad and so afraid, Rance couldn't bring herself to give her a hard time. She wasn't a hugging person, though, so she settled for awkwardly patting Moira on the shoulder until she composed herself.

Moira sniffed. "I'm glad you came, Devri."

"Better call me Rance from now on. I don't use that name anymore."

Moira nodded.

"How did you find me?" Rance asked.

Sonya swept a scanner over Rance's body, watching the screen and making little-sniffing noises herself.

"I took a chance," Moira said. "And found a dealer in the city who runs a few questionable trading routes."

"You did what? Moira, you could have run into the wrong people! They could have hurt you. How did *they* find me?"

"They didn't know you. But I paid him quite a bit of money to send my message to every known smuggling outpost in the Outer Colonies, on the off chance you were hiding on one of them. The instructions were to relay it to you."

Rance sighed. What Moira had done was extremely risky, but she was glad it had been more anonymous than she'd thought at first. Tracking a receipt at so many locations would be next to impossible. Still, she'd used Rance's real name, and Rance would bet the *Star Streaker* that whoever had sent the message had also watched the video. Moira was lucky she hadn't had something worse happen to her.

Sonya's scanner beeped, and Rance looked over.

"Nothing is wrong, Your Ladyship. You are very lucky. Are you ready to close the wound?"

"In a minute," Rance said, looking at Solaris out on the balcony. Sonya nodded and left.

Rance joined Solaris. Smoke drifted on the wind, but it wasn't so bad they couldn't enjoy the cold air.

"We need to find a way out of here," Rance said, staring at the fires that surrounded them. Thankfully, they were still at some distance. "But I don't think we can afford to keep going like we've been. We need a few hours' sleep and something to eat."

"I agree," Solaris said. "We'll make better decisions after taking a break. How's the head?"

"No real damage. Apparently, I have a very hard head."

"I already knew that, Captain." The comment was forced, not his usual light-hearted jab at all.

"What's bothering you?" she asked.

"You mean other than we've stranded ourselves in a hostile city with invading pirates and no way of communicating with the ship?"

"Yes, other than that."

Rance leaned her elbows on the railing and closed her eyes. She was so tired, but she wanted to eat. And she wanted Solaris to talk to her. Out of all her crew, he was the least transparent. She knew so little about him. Somehow it was important she knew more. Just in case one or none of them ever made it off Prometheus.

But no, she wouldn't think about that possibility.

Solaris leaned against the railing next to her and sighed. "When I was a child," he whispered, "my entire planet was destroyed by pirates."

Rance's eyes flew open. "It was? How?"

"The Galaxy Wizards never found out how they did it. But the pirates swooped in with overwhelming force and set the whole planet on fire. In the battle, it broke into pieces."

"Wow," Rance said, looking at Solaris. "How did that happen though? What kind of weapons did they use?"

"I'm not sure, but I've spent most of my life trying to figure it out. The Wizards got me off the planet. I was one of the few survivors."

"Is that how you ended up being a Wizard?"

"Yes. They raised me."

"What about your family?"

Solaris was silent, looking out over the city. "They didn't make it."

"I'm sorry," Rance breathed, horrified. She had her share of family problems, but at least she'd had a family.

"It was a long time ago. I don't remember them well."

"So that's why you've been upset."

"Correct."

Panic rose in Rance's throat. "Do you think that's going to happen here?"

"I don't know. Maybe. But I can't figure out why. My little planet was a backwater, full of pitiful farms scraped from the dust. I think the pirates had been trying to establish a base of operations there and something went wrong."

"And here?"

Solaris stood up straight and turned back toward the house. "There are all sorts of compelling reasons to control this planet, rather than destroy it."

"Let's hope you're right," Rance said. She turned to go back inside.

Solaris stopped her with a hand on her arm. "Rance?"

"Yes?"

He met her eyes. "Back on the *Streaker*, when Unity was getting ready to inspect us, you said you were a nobody."

Rance shrugged. "So?"

"You were wrong."

Heat rose to Rance's face, and she tried to clear her throat. "What brought this on?"

"Just thought you should know."

Solaris turned back out to face the fires. Rance wondered if he were worried they wouldn't make it out of their situation either. She started to put a hand on his shoulder, to let him know she appreciated his sentiment. But it felt awkward, so she dropped her hand to her side and left him on the balcony.

Inside, she went to find a room of her own. The guest rooms were as beautiful as the rest of the house, with fine artwork on the walls and soft fabrics on the bed. Rance felt at home, yet didn't. But she was too tired to consider anything other than sleep.

A moment later, Tania knocked on the door and brought a simple but fine meal of fish and fruit. Rance ate while Tania used a laser to seal the cut on the back of Rance's head. The food was good, but Rance was so hungry she wolfed it down in a few bites, without pausing to savor it.

When Tania left, Rance washed her food down with tea and eyed the luxurious sunken bath in the corner of the room. After their tough day, a hot bath would feel wonderful. But she was too tired for even that. She splashed water on her face and flopped down on the bed. It sank down with her, then automatically adjusted to her body. The bedcovers were soft and inviting, caressing her skin. With a sigh of relief, Rance drifted off.

She woke when someone tapped on her door. "Enter," she said.

The door slid open to reveal Solaris, who didn't enter but said, "Time to go, Captain."

With a groan she barely concealed, Rance rolled out of bed.

"Nice hair," Solaris smirked. Then he turned and left.

Rance rolled her eyes. Her hair, still partially braided when she'd fallen asleep, was now sticking out like a tangled nest. She unbraided it and smoothed it as best she could before twisting it together once more, finishing as she left the room.

CHAPTER EIGHT

Instead of going back outside, Moira led them down into the tower's basement. Rance tried not to think about going underground again. The panic from the day before set in quickly this time, and she took deep, calming breaths before following Moira out of the elevator. Solaris, Abel, Tania, and Sonya walked behind.

There were more residences here, small living spaces that held no more than a bunk, a galley kitchen, and a bathroom. The doors, stacked on top of one another in neat rows, resembled beehives.

"How do people get up there?" Abel asked, looking at the doors.

Moira pointed. "They have moving platforms." Small hoverboards moved up and down the walls like floating discs.

The thought of using a hoverboard to reach an underground home every night didn't sound like much fun. What if Rance accidentally stepped out the front door, and one wouldn't be there to catch her fall?

"They're for assistants or extra servants when we have guests," Moira said. "Or anyone else who wants to live in this section of the city. We're going to use the private corridors reserved for nobility. My husband uses them often when he wants to travel quickly. Normally, we'd ride a transport. But they won't be running now."

They walked down a hallway to another elevator. This one took them down five more levels, opening onto a well-lit corridor as wide as the streets above. The underground tunnel stretched up two stories and looked like a nighttime, above-ground street. On the second level, darkened windows overlooked vendors' stands and screens showing the invasion above.

It was crowded with people.

Nobles, servants, aliens. Wandering, sitting, standing. A few moved through like they had a destination in mind. Most huddled in small groups, whispering and watching the screens. A few noticed the group stepping off the elevator. Moira pulled a veil over her face.

"So this is where everyone went to," Rance said with a sinking heart. How would they get through all of this without being stopped? For once, she wished she was dressed as a noblewoman instead of a ship's captain. Their navy flight suits stood out amongst the traditional, elaborate garb of Prometheus' nobility.

Although nobility filled the halls with fine clothing, they still stank. The press of bodies, cooped up without much air flow and limited bathrooms, created a hot, sweaty odor of too many people pressed into a small space.

Underlying all of it was the scent of fear. Most people avoided eye contact with their group. Few people spoke.

Rance couldn't believe they were all just hiding. But then she realized that with so many ships destroyed, they didn't have a choice. The survivors could only hide and pray for mercy if the pirates found them.

Hiding may have been fine for all of them, but Rance had no intention of being caged like an animal.

The tunnels here were better maintained. The ceilings were higher, and lights filled every corner. It didn't feel like being underground. Rance was grateful. The situation was stressful enough without adding her claustrophobia into the mix.

They passed door after door, family after family. Rance avoided eye contact, not wishing to draw any more attention to themselves than necessary. But she often felt the stares on her back as they passed.

As they made their way to the corridor leading under the river, the crowds thinned.

"This comes up right in the Senate building," Moira said. "The offices, anyway, not the meeting hall."

"That's near the *Star Streaker*," Solaris said.

"Roote," Moira asked, "what are you carrying?"

"Just a stick I picked up." Although with a staff in hand he increased the possibility of being recognized as a Wizard, Solaris had kept it out as they walked, preferring to be on guard and armed to losing precious seconds in a fight.

Moira looked at him shrewdly, her eyebrows furrowing together beneath her veil. "I saw a man with one of those once. He came to my home with my husband."

If Solaris was surprised by this, he didn't let it show. Rance, however, had a harder time hiding her shock. A Galaxy Wizard had visited Moira's husband? What was he doing with them? Did it have something to do with his disappearance?

"It's my weapon of choice," Solaris conceded. "Although I'd rather not have to use it."

He nodded to the crowd ahead blocking the wide underground street. The atmosphere was tense.

"At least no one is fighting," Rance said.

"Yet," Solaris said. "Right now, they are like tinder waiting for a spark. It won't take much to set them on fire."

He moved ahead of the group, followed by Rance, Moira, Tania, and Sonya. Abel brought up the rear.

As Solaris moved through the crowd, it subconsciously parted for him, creating a path through. Not for the first time, Rance wished he would teach her that trick.

The group avoided eye contact with everybody. Rance shuddered to think what would happen if this crowd thought there was a ship left on Prometheus. Her crew would never make it out. She began watching the doors, looking for exits, just in case. If the crowd swarmed them, they'd need a quick escape. The only problem was knowing if a door led to a side passage or a dead end. Rance dropped back to walk beside Moira.

"Do you know another route, if we need it?" she whispered.

"I know a couple, but I've really only ever used this one."

"Are they easy to get to?"

"Yes. Several of these side passages take you to other underground streets. It's laid out on a grid."

Rance wished the other tunnels they'd used had been laid out on a grid. But then, service tunnels were always different. They passed one of the passages Moira had described. An alley, leading out to another well-lit thorough-fare. She nudged Solaris, who took note.

After that, Rance kept her eyes peeled. Above them, the ground occasionally shook, as if the pirates were bombing the city. Every time a roll of thunder pealed over the street, the crowd ducked. The group moved faster. The *Star Streaker* was hidden, not impervious. If they didn't hurry, they might not have a ship to return to.

Rance's heart pounded in her throat, and the urgency of their situation grew with each shudder of the ceiling above. Then, one particularly violent shake felt like an earthquake, and the lights flickered. A few people screamed. More families began moving about. A few followed Rance's group. She tried not to glance back at them. They were probably just using the same route to get out. But she couldn't help but wonder if they were following because they wanted to see where Rance and her crew were going.

They had just passed another alley when a familiar woman stepped out from around the corner. She wore cream-colored robes and a jewel-encrusted headpiece. She locked eyes with Rance, and then her gaze slid back to Moira. Rance groaned as recognition flashed in the woman's eyes.

"Moira?" she asked.

Rance and Moira stopped walking. Sensing trouble, Solaris kept his back to Moira and watched the crowd. Rance did the same, keeping Moira and the woman in her peripheral vision. In addition to watching the crowd, she had another reason for not making eye contact with the woman.

Rance knew Lady Lysa. The woman was from Xanthes, had dined in her father's home. She was also responsible for pressuring Rance's father, Davos, to arrange Rance's marriage to Harrison McConnell.

"Hello, Lysa," Moira said.

"I thought you'd left Prometheus with your husband?" Lysa asked.

She looked at Moira's company, sweeping her eyes up and down Solaris' flight suit. Her gaze slid over Rance, then Tania. "And you've got your servants with you, I see."

"I couldn't leave them behind. You know how indispensable they are to me, Lysa. I can't even go into hiding without them." Moira smiled, but it looked forced.

"And this flight crew?"

"Friends."

Rance prayed Moira didn't mention her real name. Even now, she didn't want Davos to find out she'd been on Prometheus. If she escaped the pirates, Lysa would report straight to him.

"If I didn't know you were helpless without your husband, I would think you were planning to fly away."

Moira's face blushed so red Rance could see the color beneath her veil. "I am not helpless without my husband. And we aren't flying anywhere. It's hard to do that without a ship. Now, if you'll pardon us, we're going to find a quiet hallway away from this infernal crowd."

Lysa nodded. The group moved on, faster than before. But when Rance glanced back, Lysa was following close behind Abel.

Rance nudged Solaris again and whispered, "We've got a problem."

"She's following?"

"Yes."

Moira had looked back too, and seeing Lysa, stopped to confront her.

Rance grabbed her arm. "No, keep moving."

Moira obeyed, and they turned once again, walking faster. Rance began to scan the area, looking for a side street to run down if they needed to. But Lysa was following too closely for them to make an easy getaway.

The crowd noticed the group, watching with interest as they flashed by. As Solaris picked up the pace, Lysa fell behind.

"Wait!" she called.

More curious eyes, more piercing stares.

Rance sped up, moving up to Solaris' elbow. Behind her, Moira stumbled, and Tania steadied her.

"This is going to get bad," Rance said. "Get us out of here."

Solaris nodded. "Yes, Captain."

He turned aside so quickly he almost ran her over. They darted down a side alley.

But Lysa wasn't going to get lost so easily. "You have a ship!" she yelled at their backs.

"No," Rance whispered, hoping no one had heard Lysa.

But the crowd had heard her. One by one, nobles and servants looked at the group running down the alley. And then, as one, they followed. Lysa put on a burst of speed and caught up to them. Abel grabbed her arm and shoved her back.

She fought him, kicking and scratching. It didn't do any

good against his armor, but it drew even more attention. Behind, the crowd grew closer.

"Moira!" Lysa called. "You can't leave us here! Take me with you!"

Moira turned.

Rance grabbed her arm. "No! Keep moving!"

"We can't take anybody with us," Moira whined. "I'm sorry!"

Rance groaned.

"Let's get out of here," Solaris said through gritted teeth. He grabbed Moira's left arm, Rance grabbed her right, and they marched her down the alley. Abel had released Lysa, but the woman followed. So did the growing crowd.

Lysa fell in with the followers, making sure they heard her loud and clear. "They have a ship! They're going to leave us here to die!"

Moira burst into tears, dragging her feet and forcing Rance and Solaris to pull her along.

"Keep it together, Moira," Rance hissed. "We can't do anything for them. We don't have room. Do you want to stay here and die with them? Huh?"—she shook her friend—"Sacrifice yourself for the people that turned a blind eye when your husband disappeared?"

Those were the wrong words. Moira moaned loudly and tried to turn around.

Solaris pulled Moira close. "So help me, Your Ladyship, we will drag you out of here if we have to. We came to this stinking planet to save you, and that's what we're going to do."

Moira tried to pull away from him, but his grip on her arm remained firm.

"But if you endanger my friends any more than you already have," he continued. "I'll leave you here to deal with the pirates that are this *minute* occupying the city. Is that clear?"

Rance wanted to argue with him, but she couldn't. She felt the same way. And that Solaris valued her and Abel's lives enough to say so made her heart swell with pride, despite her growing anxiety about the crowd.

And then they came to the end of the alley.

Another group had gathered, blocking their exit. Drawn by the noise of the crowd behind, they looked curiously at the six people running away from an increasingly angry mob.

They were trapped. To the left, one door read *Stairs*. Without thinking, Rance steered her charge for it, hoping it wasn't locked.

The crowds, sensing their prey was about to get away, charged. Rance didn't even have time to wonder what they'd do if they caught them. She waved her hand over the sensor at the door, and it swung open. The group fell through the doorway as one, jostling each other into a dark, narrow entry-way. Solaris turned and locked the door behind them with a tap of his staff.

The structure shuddered with the onslaught above, and the stairs groaned. On reflex, everyone looked up the dark stairway.

Outside the door, someone screamed.

"Tania!" Sonya yelled in answer.

Rance looked around—Tania wasn't there. She'd been shut out.

Moira began crying afresh, and Sonya whimpered like a lost child.

"Everybody PULL YOURSELVES TOGETHER!" Rance yelled.

Startled, they stopped crying long enough to look at her.

Rance dropped her bag on the floor and then unholstered her blaster. Abel already had one in each hand.

"Stay here," Rance commanded Moira. "We'll be back in five minutes."

Moira grabbed Rance's sleeve, pinching her arm hard. "Don't go out there!"

Sonya grabbed Moira. "We can't leave Tania!"

"Let go of me, servant!"

"Enough," Solaris said. With one hand, he separated the women. Then he nodded to Rance. "Count of three. One, two, three."

He tapped the door again, and it burst inward—the crowd had been pressing against it. Surprised, the people closest pulled out of the doorway. With the door open, Rance saw the desperation and malice in their eyes. This crowd was terrified—they would kill all of them before they realized what they were doing.

Abel pushed his way out the door, and when the blood-crazed crowd saw his weapons pointed at their faces, they halted. From somewhere to the right, Tania shrieked again.

"Give us the girl," Abel said. "Now."

"Take us with you!" someone screamed. Lysa had disappeared.

When they didn't back off, Abel leveled his blaster at the man standing closest. The man's eyes grew wide.

"I am asking nicely," Abel said.

But the rest of the crowd, indifferent to what happened to

the man, began shouting. The din bounced off the close walls and into the stairwell.

Rance scanned the crazed mob, looking for Tania. They needed to find her before something worse happened. The earth rumbled again, this time so violently Rance grabbed the door frame to keep from being thrown off her feet.

But instead of fading away, the trembling grew more brutal. Rance's teeth chattered so much she had to clamp her mouth shut to keep from breaking them all off. The alleyway ceiling began to crumble, and the mob scattered, screaming.

Then the alley exploded in a flash of light. People flew backward, smacking against walls and crumpling on top of one another. The pressure forced Rance backward, but the middle of the alley had sustained the worst of the blast.

At first, Rance thought Solaris had attacked the mob like he had the soldiers on Doxor 5. But he stood next to her, blocking the doorway behind Abel.

She looked up. The explosion had come from the ceiling where sparks rained down on the alley below. Whole chunks of the ceiling had collapsed, causing something above to explode and ignite.

Fire licked down through a great hole. Below, people moaned and began getting to their feet. A few lay still, but Rance ran past them, looking for Tania.

She had been held farther away, out of the line of the blast. At the disturbance, the crowd had let her loose. Rance jumped over two bodies and grabbed her hand.

"You okay?"

Tania nodded, and Rance pulled her along, trying not to look at who or what they were stepping over.

The ceiling groaned and shifted, like the supports above

would give way at any moment. A blaring alarm sounded, and soon the place was buzzing with drones and androids sent to assess the problem and put out the fire.

But everyone could see that the alley was going to collapse. The mob had scattered, leaving the way clear for Rance and Tania. They ran through the door to the stairwell, and Abel closed it behind. Solaris sealed it for good measure.

Sonya grabbed Tania and held her tight while glaring daggers at Moira. The noblewoman had the sense to look embarrassed and avoided everyone else's gaze. She sank down against the wall and put her head on her knees.

Everyone took a moment to breathe. The stairwell shook again, but Rance sat down on the third step and looked at Solaris.

"What are they doing up there?"

"Sounds like they're attacking the residential district now," Solaris said, looking up the stairwell with a frown. "Although I have no idea why. You'd think they'd attack something more strategic, like the Unity base or the Senate building.

"It is a symbol of extravagance, boss," Abel said. He may have been a hulk, but Abel could be surprisingly astute when it suited him. "That is why they're attacking it."

"Better that than the Senate building," Rance said. "We left the *Star Streaker* not too far away from it."

"That is my home!" Moira said suddenly. She raised her head, and her red-rimmed, puffy eyes made her look older and more destitute.

"*Was* your home," Solaris said. He'd lost all patience with her, it seemed.

"Where to from here?" Rance asked, standing and

dusting off her hands. "We still need to go under the river, correct? We haven't done that yet?"

Moira shook her head.

"So we are back to the tunnels," Abel said. "Come on. I'll lead the way."

He helped Tania to her feet, and they walked up the flight of stairs, which emptied them out into a service tunnel. They had to choose left or right. Rance had completely lost her sense of direction, and when she called upon her NNR to show her a map, all she got was static in her ZOD. It *would* have picked that moment to glitch out. They still had Abel's HUD, so he took point and led them to the service network. They headed down a corridor, and then descended two flights of narrow, metal stairs to end in another service tunnel.

The new tunnels looked much like the tunnels they'd used the day before—dirty, greasy, and smelly. More signs of an empire degrading. Only this time, Rance kept her eyes on each door they passed, half-expecting an angry mob to burst out of one and block their exit. All the doors looked alike, except for a few with red or yellow signs plastered in a language Rance didn't know. If her NNR had been working, she could have translated without trouble.

Abel didn't have any trouble deciphering it because he used it to navigate as they went.

"What do they mean?" Rance asked after the fifth door.

Abel shrugged. "Just numbers."

Rance's heart was still beating fast from the encounter below. And her senses were hyper-aware. She couldn't relax. Really, she didn't want to. The adrenaline rush was all that was keeping the guilt at bay. She mentally ticked off all the reasons for hating herself. One, they'd left all those people behind. Two, Rance had endangered her crew on the most foolish errand imaginable. Three, they had no plan for escaping the planet, other than taking off and hoping for the best.

Don't think about it now.

But she couldn't stop thinking about it. She tugged at her collar again, but since she still wore her helmet, no air passed through her suit. She kept her visor up and plodded on. The tunnels were uncomfortably warm, and after a minute Rance realized the air flow had stopped.

"I'm surprised we still have power," she commented.

"These underground tunnels have their own grid," Abel said. "But it's probably in jeopardy like everything else."

With the absence of ventilation, they grew stifling hot. Rance sweated through her flight suit, which was designed to wick away moisture. But it couldn't keep up with the heat. Soon, the fabric mesh lining was so wet it stuck to her skin and began chafing.

So much for state-of-the-art flight suits. Rance made a mental note to get different ones if they ever got out of this mess. As they walked, the adrenaline rush abated. The guilt hit her full force, washing over her in wave after wave. Raised around perfection and with high standards, Rance had always been hard on herself when she messed up.

And she'd really messed up this time.

They walked a long time, following Abel's cues. Moira, Tania, and Sonya remained quiet. Once Rance had calmed down, she felt sorry for all three of them. They'd always lived around comfort, even the servants, and had never been in a life-threatening situation such as this.

But Rance was still disgusted with herself for even being in this situation.

In addition to the guilt overwhelming her, every inch of Rance's body was bone-tired. She pinched herself to keep from falling asleep as she walked.

Soon, the tunnel began to stink. She closed her visor and let her suit's air circulate. But the battery was low—it wouldn't last much longer.

Everything began to look alike. The walls, the doors, the signs. The red and yellow became blurred. Rance raised her visor and pushed her palms into her eyes, trying to wake up.

They didn't stop until an hour later when they sagged against a wall to rest. Rance leaned her head back against the inside of her helmet. But she couldn't get comfortable, so she removed the helmet to let some air to her head.

The stench of the tunnel drove her to put it right back on. So much for some air. Rance looked over at Moira, whose dress hem was stained with the filth of the tunnel and whose nose was permanently wrinkled at the stink. The veil did nothing to protect her from it. As Rance watched, Moira removed the fine veil and cast it aside. It fell onto the greasy floor without ceremony.

They all looked worse for wear. Abel's eyes were puffy. Solaris looked paler than Rance had ever seen, and Tania and Sonya looked so tired, they might have been sleep-walking.

If they stayed any longer, they'd fall asleep, and possibly lose their window for leaving the planet—if they still had one. With a groan, Rance climbed to her feet and gave the command to move out. No one complained aloud, but everyone glared at her. One by one, they stood and moved on down the tunnel.

The rumbling above subsided as they marched downward, under the river. Rance prayed the explosions above hadn't damaged the tunnels so badly they would flood. She could think of more horrible deaths than violent drowning, but not many.

As they moved deeper under the river, the water streaming down the walls became more than condensation. Soon they were sloshing through water up to their ankles, and Rance was thankful for her tall boots.

The water ran downhill toward the lowest portion of the tunnel. It washed the floor grease on top, creating little rainbow-colored rivers of oil on top of the new current.

The group halted.

"What's the final depth under the river?" Solaris asked Abel.

He shook his head. "Dunno. But we go quite a bit deeper than this before it slopes upward."

They needed to choose. Go forward until the water became too powerful to deal with? Or go back and find an alternate route?

"Regardless of which tunnel we use," Rance said. "We need to cross the river. I don't know how we're going to do that above ground."

"Right," Abel said, frowning. "Right."

They all stared at the water a minute. Rance was hoping for a genius idea, a moment of inspiration. She didn't care who came up with it as long as it got them out of their predicament. When no one spoke, she realized they were waiting on her to make the decision.

"Down," she said finally. "At least this way we might have a chance. Up top, we have nothing."

They nodded, and the group continued on. The farther they traveled, the deeper the water became. When it first spilled over the top of Rance's boots, she gasped at the cold. Then she glanced back at Moira and her servants, who had been walking through the icy water without complaint all this time.

Rance felt another twinge of guilt, but she couldn't do anything about it. The options remained the same—go back up to be stuck in the apocalypse, or continue their current path and cross the river.

When the water level was thigh-high, they moved to the wall to steady themselves. At this depth, Rance could still push through, but Moira and the other women were struggling. It was up to their waists and occasionally lifted them off their feet. Abel was shorter than Rance and Solaris, but his massive, armored body had no trouble staying grounded. He held out an arm for their wards to cling to, staying behind them to buffer the worst of the current.

When Rance lifted her visor to let some air into her suit, water splashed onto her face. It stank but cooled her face.

"How much farther, you think?" she yelled over the roar of the water.

"We've got to be close!" Solaris answered. "If we're not, the current is going to wash us away!"

As they braced themselves against the current, the lights began to flicker. Then, Rance heard the noise she'd been dreading.

A rumbling sound overcame the sound of rushing water. She turned and looked back up the tunnel from where they'd come. With a sinking feeling, she noticed the lights behind them had gone out completely. The noise grew beyond a roar, more like a tempest.

The tunnel was flooding.

"Everybody grab onto something!" she screamed, grabbing a pitifully small door handle.

She barely got the words out of her mouth when a wall of water hit them from behind.

CHAPTER NINE

IF RANCE HAD EVER FALLEN out of an air vehicle without a parachute, she imagined this is what hitting the ground would feel like. All the air was knocked out of her, and her body smacked into Solaris, who was standing in front of her when the water hit.

Her hand was yanked away from the door, and sharp pain shot up her arm as two fingers were dislocated. Rance yelped and gulped a mouthful of water.

Then her entire body was underwater, the current pulling and pushing, slamming her against the wall, against another person—she couldn't tell who at this point—and even into the piping along the ceiling.

Time seemed to slow. Rance had never felt so much pain in her life. Every part of her body was being pummeled, and she'd never been so grateful for a helmet as she was at that moment, even if she'd been caught with the visor open.

But even as Rance registered that she was still alive, she waited for her death. She was powerless to stop her body from rolling over and over in the current, from banging against every object imaginable. And she needed *air*.

Her lungs were about to burst. Any second, her body would force her mouth open to take great lungfuls of greasy, black water. She'd always thought she'd die in space—in a glorious space battle or as an old woman in her chair, watching the stars slide by. Drowning underground had never been an option.

If she stopped fighting, it would all be over. The pain in her body and lungs would vanish. If she'd just let go.

Still rolling over and over, Rance allowed her arms to float out to her side, preparing to give in.

And then a hand grabbed hers. Its grip was strong, and it almost dislocated her arm as it pulled her through the water. As soon as she realized what was happening, she fought harder to hold her breath.

It became harder than ever. Her lungs were going to burst. She had to breathe.

The next second, Rance was hauled up into a pocket of air. She gasped. The icy water tugged angrily at her body, the current trying to reclaim its prize. Someone grabbed her by the neck of her suit and pulled until she banged against something thin and metal—a pipe. She grabbed onto it in the darkness, holding on to save her life.

Then, the person was gone.

Rance sputtered and gasped. She must have inhaled water at some point because her chest burned. The metal pipe she was holding had a twin at her elbow. Another was at her knee.

They weren't pipes. It was a ladder.

She climbed up, hauling her bruised and battered body

out of the water. Before her boots were clear, somebody else burst out of the water. No, *two* somebodies.

"Hey!" she called, groping down to grab someone. She found hair and pulled anyway.

Solaris yelped. "Watch it! I'm trying to save people here!"

Rance let go. "Sorry! Here, give me somebody!"

Solaris hoisted the other sputtering person onto the ladder. By the sound of it, he'd found Moira.

"I've got you, Moira!" Rance said. "Hang on and let's get up higher!" Rance was already shaking with cold, but her heart chilled more as she thought of Abel, Tania, and Sonya.

"Abel has Tania and Sonya," Solaris said, anticipating her question.

Rance sagged against the ladder in relief. Moira pressed herself against Rance's legs, shaking like a wet kitten.

"Move up," Solaris said. "I'm freezing."

They climbed up farther. Rance was shaking so badly now with cold that she had trouble holding onto the ladder. Her left hand slipped, sending more pain through her dislocated fingers.

"Okay, I'm good," Solaris said. "We're out of the water. Okay, Moira?"

Moira had yet to say anything, but she whimpered through chattering teeth. Then she sniffed and asked, "What h-happened to T-Tania and Sonya?"

"Abel's got them on another ladder," Solaris said. "I spotted these maintenance shafts just as the water hit us. I almost had you, Rance, but then the water tore you away from me. The next person to hit me was Abel, so I grabbed him and pointed him toward the ladder. With his suit, he had been swimming around, searching for us. Then we went after everybody else. That man can swim like a lantess, even in armor."

"How do you know they got into the other ladder?"

"That shaft has light. I saw them. Unfortunately, we're going to have to climb this one in the dark."

"Better than being too dead to climb anything," Rance said.

Without further conversation, she began climbing. Rance had always preferred action to sitting around pondering, and they had nowhere to go but up. Her back scraped along the rear wall, and she silently cursed the short maintenance crew. She engaged her magnetic boots and used them to steady herself on the metal ladder. The going was easier after that, but her thighs were soon burning with the effort. With no light to gauge distance, and barely enough room to squeeze through, she felt as if she were climbing a never-ending tunnel. Before long, her heart was pounding along with the burn in her legs.

And still they climbed. Rance hoped they came out in the same place as Abel and the others, then realized that unless the other tunnel went sideways, they would end up just down from them. The thought cheered her and motivated her to keep climbing.

Below, Moira was struggling. Her breath came in gasps, her tears came in gushes, but she didn't ask them to stop. Occasionally, Solaris called up to her, alternating between encouragement and threats.

Rance's leg muscles moved from burning to cramping. Her bruised body ached with every step, and even breathing hurt. She thought she might have cracked a rib. She knew she'd broken at least one finger. And then they still had no idea how far they had to climb.

Just when she felt like she couldn't go any further, she banged the top of her skull against something metal. It rang with the blow. "Son of *Triton*," she said. "I think we're at the top."

"And?" Solaris asked.

"Hang on a minute." Rance fumbled her cold, numb fingers around on the metal, looking for a handle or latch. Then she found it—a recessed handle near the ladder. She managed to get her fingers underneath it and pulled.

Nothing.

She yanked on it as hard as she dared without breaking anything else.

Still nothing.

"For the love of the Founders, it won't budge."

"Did you try pushing?" Solaris asked.

"Of course I..." No. She hadn't tried that. Rance pulled the handle and simultaneously pushed up with as much strength as she could muster. Her ribs ached. Every bit of her body protested.

And then the door popped open.

The first thing Rance noticed was fresh air on her face. The next thing she noticed was the light. It was night, but after climbing up a black tunnel, the little light up top was as good as daylight. Rance resisted the urge to whoop for joy and climbed out.

She sprawled out on the ground, facing the sky, and

relished stretching her legs and her cramped, sore body. Moira came out next and crawled away from the manhole to sit against a tree.

Then Solaris appeared. Even in the dim light, Rance saw his bloody, bruised face. He must not have had his helmet on when the water hit them. She couldn't remember now. He heaved himself out of the tunnel and lay on his back beside her, breathing heavily.

They were silent a minute, then Rance whispered, "Thanks for coming to get me."

Solaris laughed and then moaned with pain. "As always, Captain, you're my ride. What would I do without you?"

"Did you get into this much trouble with the Wizards?"

"It's a close tie, I think."

"Seriously, I thought I was gone," she said. She needed him to know. "Thank you."

"You're welcome."

They lay in silence a bit longer, savoring the feeling of freedom and life. Then a horrible thought occurred to Rance. "What side of the river are we on?"

"Don't know. I'm just glad we're not underneath it."

But Solaris sat up—carefully—and looked around. Then he looked up at the sky. "I think we're in the Senate section. This street looks familiar."

Rance sat up too, looking around at the wide street lined with trees. "How can you tell?"

"He's right, Devri," Moira said.

Rance jerked around at her name, and then sharp pain shot through her neck, and she wished she hadn't. "Rance," she corrected.

"Rance," Moira said. "We made it."

"Not yet we haven't," Solaris said grimly as he climbed to his feet. He held out a hand for Rance, who was too tired to refuse his help. When she gripped his hand, she noticed his skin was unnaturally smooth. It didn't have the usual calluses and ridges he'd had there before now. Then she was on her feet, and he let go.

As they attempted to get their bearings, three starships sped by overhead, weaving among the tall buildings.

"Pirates," Solaris said, watching the sky. "Looks like they've begun landing in earnest."

"Then we're out of time," Rance said. "We've got to find Abel and get out."

"Abel will meet us at the ship."

"I'm not leaving until we see them climb up out of the ground!"

"Captain, Abel is armed to the teeth and wearing combat armor, and those girls are tough. They're probably already on their way."

But Rance insisted on searching the area, so they fanned out, looking for another manhole. One street over, they found one just like theirs. It was open, the light shining all the way down as far as they could see.

"This has to be it," Solaris said. "Now can we go to the ship?"

"Alright, I had to be sure."

"Your loyalty is admirable, Captain."

"I don't know any other way to be," Rance muttered.

They hurried along, looking for any recognizable land-marks. Finally, they found a street they'd used a day ago. Rance could hardly believe it had taken that long to get back here. But her tired, bruised body reminded her at every step.

After they had turned down the street, they encountered crowds of wanderers fleeing other parts of the city. Although they couldn't see the fires, smoke drifted around the buildings on the wind. More ships passed overhead, cruising slowly now. They followed the crowds, heading in the same general direction.

"Wonder where they're all heading?" Rance asked.

"The Senate building, looks like," Moira said.

They still hadn't seen Abel, Tania, or Sonya. Rance kept her eyes on the crowds, in part to find Abel, and in part to spot trouble.

"At least the sirens aren't blaring anymore."

They passed a working screen taking up the whole side of a building. It displayed footage of the pirates landing, along with a message to go to the Senate.

"No reason, though," Solaris said. "That doesn't bode well."

"Looks like people are doing it."

"They don't have much choice. Their homes were burned."

Rance swallowed the fear building and concentrated on their goal—to get to the *Star Streaker*. She opened a private channel and tried hailing James again. Just as before—no answer, not even static. Her comm must have busted in the tunnel below. If only Rance could talk to him, she'd feel better. She sighed and walked as fast as her body would allow.

They saw the first group of pirates in the street, herding Prometheus' citizens toward the Senate building. Rance, Solaris, and Moira stayed in the middle of the crowd, careful not to make eye contact with anyone. They weren't likely to be recognized, but they didn't want to be stopped, either.

Rance wondered what had happened to all the people below. Had water burst through everywhere? She doubted it. The river would have only flooded some of the most damaged sections. Would the pirates go down there and get people out? Probably. Eventually. When all that was left would be bodies.

Finally, the crowd bottlenecked in the street, and Rance peered over heads to see what was happening.

"We've got a problem," she said a minute later. "Check-point. They're making people identify themselves."

"How?"

"Looks like retinal scan."

"Fantastic," Solaris said in a voice that indicated he thought it anything but.

"Oh no," Moira said. She hadn't spoken in over an hour.

"What?" Rance asked.

"They can't figure out who I am." She gripped Rance's sleeve again. Rance winced. Her sore body needed to be handled gently, not pinched.

"They don't need to figure out who any of us are," Rance said, thinking of her father and the ten million credits he would pay anybody who found his daughter, pirate or no.

"You don't understand, Dev—Rance. My husband was quite outspoken against the pirates. He supported torture and the death penalty for them. If they find out who I am—"

Rance glanced at Moira, who seemed about to hyperventilate again, and whispered to Solaris, "Will a retina scan reveal your true identity?"

Solaris took a deep breath. "I can disguise us. All of us. It won't be easy though. And once I do that, I'll be too drained to fight much. I still haven't fully recovered from our landing."

"Our *magical* landing. As soon as we get out of this, I want you to tell me how you did that."

"If I told you exactly how your eyes would glaze over."

"Try me, just once."

"Okay, I will. When we get out of this mess."

"Deal."

Feeling calmer, Rance strode ahead through the crowd, keeping an eye out for Abel. Finally, she spotted him standing next to Tania at the edge of the crowd.

"About time," she said, and elbowed her way through disgruntled noblemen and their assistants.

Abel's weapons had disappeared. Like everyone else, his face was bloodied and bruised—how had that happened inside his helmet? His armor had huge dents in it. Likely they would have to pry him out of it later. Tania was pale and quietly held onto his arm.

"Abel!" Rance said, smiling.

Abel forced a smile when he saw her. "Hey, boss."

Rance ducked her head to whisper, "Roote is going to disguise us to get through. Where's Sonya?"

Abel's face paled. Tania stifled a sob.

"She didn't make it, boss."

"Didn't make it?" Rance repeated, not sure she'd heard him correctly. A cold feeling washed over her. Moira covered her mouth with her hand. Solaris' mouth pressed into a thin, hard line.

"I found her, but I was too late." Abel cleared his throat. "She drowned."

Rance's eyes stung. Solaris had said they'd all got out. He'd been sure. A flash of anger shot through her, but she had nowhere to direct it.

Except at the pirates who were shouting at people to get a move on.

Abel looked horrified at the expression on Rance's face. "I'm sorry, boss."

"Not your fault, Abel."

"If only we'd been faster—" Solaris began.

"It's not your fault, either!" Rance snarled. "It's their fault!"

She pointed at the pirates while her vision blurred at the edges. She didn't know if it was the tears or her anger.

Solaris pulled out his staff and flicked it out to its full length. "They are a menace to the empire, but we cannot fight them here and now. Rance," he pleaded, "we have to get out of here."

But Rance's face only grew hotter. The pirates were responsible for all of it. For the destruction of a beautiful city, for the death of an innocent woman. Prometheus may have had its share of corruption, but plenty of good, peaceful people lived here. How many had died? How many more would die before the nightmare was over?

"Devri," Solaris whispered.

That got her attention. "I told you, don't—"

"Look at me, please."

Rance glared at him.

Solaris put a hand on each shoulder. His hands were warm, heavy. "You won't avenge Sonya's death by getting yourself killed. I know a bit about this, remember? Breathe."

As he whispered the last word, an intense calm washed

over Rance, and she felt like she had no choice but to do as he said. She took a few deep, calming breaths, expelling the anger from her body.

"What did you do to me?"

"Just something you wanted to do for yourself but couldn't."

Solaris was doing the same thing he'd done to Turkey. But he couldn't be. She still knew where she was, still recognized her surroundings. Rance stared at Solaris.

The crowd jostled past, and someone bumped Rance's shoulder. She winced in pain, suddenly aware again of others around her. Solaris removed his hands, then grabbed his staff. In a moment's work, all five of them looked like completely different people. Even Solaris looked shorter than usual. Rance remembered him telling her that he never disguised his height because it took a lot of energy.

He was already draining his power. She couldn't let it go to waste.

So, she pushed through the crowd, toward the checkpoint. The first guard waved her over. He was a brutish, smelly young man who would have been good looking if he'd had a bath recently. He held a small scanner up to Rance's eyes and waited.

The scanner beeped, and a light turned green. "Varea ar noll," he said. "City cleaner. Cleared."

Rance had no idea who Varea ar noll was, nor how Solaris had stolen her retinal signature, but she breathed a sigh of relief as she stepped through the checkpoint. The others followed behind. Solaris, the last to be cleared, looked drawn and haggard.

Once clear, they hurried down the street, turning aside from the rest of the crowd, toward the *Star Streaker*.

"Hey!" someone called.

Rance glanced back and grimaced. One of the pirates had noticed them split off from the main crowd. He waved at them to move back into line. She pretended like she hadn't seen him and kept walking.

But Abel, who had a rear camera in his helmet, said, "They're following."

With her injuries, Rance didn't think she had the energy left to run. But when she looked back at the pirates and saw them running after them, she burst into a run too. The others followed.

More shouts from behind. With the effort to breathe, Rance's ribs felt like they were trying to burst out her skin. She stumbled, but Abel caught her and they kept going. Then, he turned. Rance saw him stop and plant himself in the middle of the street behind the crew, preparing to face the pirates alone so the others could get away.

"No!" she cried and stopped with him. Moira and Tania ran past.

Solaris caught Rance's arm to stop her from going after Abel.

"Let go!"

"I got him," Solaris said. And then without another word, he ran toward the pirates, wielding his staff above his head like a two-handed sword. When he passed Abel, he swung the staff. This time, no purple bubble appeared, no visible wall of energy.

But the pirates were thrust backward like they'd been hit

with a wrecking ball. They flew down the street and landed in a heap near the crowd. None of them moved. And Rance knew that without armor, few people could survive a blow like that.

Without waiting to find out the pirates' fates, Solaris and Abel joined the others. They turned down a side street. As soon as they rounded the corner, they assumed their normal appearances. Although Solaris' usual face wasn't his true one, he adopted the usual disguise. His left eye was still swollen although the cut above his eyebrow had finally stopped bleeding. He panted heavily, his face ghostly white.

After getting her bearings, Rance assumed the lead. The *Streaker* was close, next to a park. She wouldn't be able to see it if it were still disguised, but she remembered the tall, dark-faced building they'd landed next to. She scanned the area for a sign.

Then, she saw the building. No ship. Even though her brain told her it was hidden, her heart stopped at the sight of an empty place in front of the building. She held her breath.

"Is it still there?" she asked.

Solaris waved his hand, and the *Star Streaker* appeared in front of the building, intact and ready to go.

CHAPTER TEN

THE BEAUTIFUL BRONZE ship was the most welcome sight Rance had ever seen. Lit by the glow of a fire two streets over, her home shone even in the darkness. She checked the vicinity for trouble, but the way was clear. As they hurried to the ship, Solaris stumbled. Rance caught his arm and hauled him up. If only they could get to the door without trouble.

"Okay?" she asked. Although she supported Solaris, she too was about to collapse.

"Yep."

But Solaris didn't look okay, and Rance realized he'd been draining his power the entire time the ship had been disguised. For a whole day. Rance vowed to find better ways to disguise the crew in the future. Then she decided that in the future, she wouldn't take on any jobs where disguises were required.

If they got out of this alive, she was going to start transporting illegal cappatters. No one attacked you for delivering squealing, cuddly pets.

As they reached the ship, the ramp lowered. Rance's heart was beating loudly. They were almost home. Almost safe.

With almost everybody. Her heart wrenched when she saw Tally peering at them with his large, glowing green eyes. They stumbled onto the *Streaker*, collapsing onto the floor of the cargo bay. Rance kissed the cold metal for good measure. Then she rolled onto her back and looked up at Tally.

"Tell James to get us out of here, Tally."

But Tally didn't move. He always acknowledged her. Always. But now he stood there looking at Rance like he was afraid to tell her something. She propped herself up on her elbows.

"Tally? Where's James?"

"He went out after Harper. I'd be out there too, but someone needed to be here if you needed help." He looked at Moira. "Good to see you, my Lady."

"And you, Tally."

Solaris stood wearily to his feet. Rance hadn't thought he had enough strength left, but he leaned on his staff and asked, "Why did Harper leave?"

"She was trying to figure out a way to boost communications. We wanted to be able to fly to you once you found Lady Moira."

Rance struggled to stand. Every muscle in her body protested. But the panic she felt now tripled as she realized they'd have to go back out.

Solaris and Abel seemed to be thinking the same thing. Abel moved to the weapons locker to replace the ones he'd lost.

"I told everyone to stay on board!" Rance yelled as she

went to get a gun of her own. For good measure, she grabbed two daggers and attached them with a belt.

"Yes, but Harper said she could get through the pirates' jammers if she found the right spot on that building."

Rance mashed the button to lower the ramp again. When it landed, she stomped off the ship. Abel and Solaris followed.

Out on the street, they fanned out once again, this time heading for the dark tower nearby.

"What was she thinking?" Rance fumed.

"She was trying to help, boss," Abel said.

"She disobeyed a direct order," Solaris said.

"Oh stuff it, *Roote*. This isn't Unity." Rance immediately chastised herself for losing her patience with Solaris. He was right. Harper had defied her even though it was to help.

"What do you think?" she asked after a minute. "Inside, or around?"

"If she was trying to get around the jammers, she would have wanted to go to the top of the building," Solaris said.

"Then that's what we'll do."

They hurried for the front steps, Solaris raising his staff in preparation for unlocking the door. Just then, someone yelled from an alleyway to the left.

Rance halted mid stride, listening. Abel nearly collided with her. Then she heard it again—a defiant cry, joined now by catcalling voices. As one, Rance, Solaris, and Abel changed course for the alley. As soon as they rounded the corner, Rance thanked her lucky stars they'd arrived when they did.

Harper was backed against a wall, her eyes scanning the faces of five men in front of her. Already a petite woman, she looked tiny in the shadow of the pirate thugs who carried small arms and lead pipes.

Harper's eyes flashed in defiance as they closed in. She crouched low, ready to sprint for any opening they might give her.

Rance was furious, her tunnel vision returning. This time, she doubted Solaris would try to stop her from murdering the pirate scumbags. With the return of the tunnel vision, all weariness left her body, and her head cleared, ready for a fight. She checked her daggers, then raised her gun.

Rance, Solaris, and Abel charged at once. Time slowed for Rance, who had been in a handful of conflicts where she'd had to fight for her life. This one was different. They were fighting for someone else. She'd already lost one person in her charge tonight. She wouldn't lose another.

The pirates heard the oncoming storm and turned to face their attackers. Rance's Academy training kicked in, and she fired on the first who raised his blaster. Her shot hit him squarely in the chest, and he flew backward into the brick wall, narrowly missing Harper. The other four fired together, but Solaris generated a quick shield and blocked their fire. He sent out a burst of energy that sent them reeling back, their guns flying out of their hands. The shield wasn't as powerful as he'd used on the pirates half an hour ago, but it allowed them to get to Harper.

Solaris was too tired to do more. Rance wasn't going to see him get hurt, either. He'd already done enough.

So Rance led the charge, yelling a battle cry as she met

the first pirate head on. She didn't want to risk shooting Harper, so she hit the brute with the butt end of her rifle, knocking out two teeth just as he swiped at her with a massive fist. She dodged him and spun around to knock him in the kidney. He grunted but turned and came after her.

The others joined in the fray, even Harper, who'd thrown herself onto a pirate's back and was trying to choke him. Rance lost track of who was fighting whom and concentrated on hitting anything that wasn't wearing a navy flight suit.

The first pirate rapped her hand with his fist, and Rance winced when her dislocated fingers popped back into place.

She smiled. "Thanks," she said and brought her knee up to connect with his groin.

The man doubled over. Rance launched herself at him, refusing to give him breathing space. One blow with her rifle, two blows, and he fell back, unconscious. She hesitated, tempted to finish him off. After all, they had taken Sonya.

But the ongoing fight drew her attention. Two more pirates were still up. Harper had been thrown off to the side, but she was getting to her feet as well. Solaris, clearly fighting fatigue, still managed to avoid his pirate's jabs. Then, he found an opening and whacked the man on the head with his staff.

The pirate went down, laying still on the pavement.

That left one more. The four advanced on him, backing him against the wall. Rance raised her blaster and aimed it at his forehead. The blood-lust that had come over her was still coursing through her body, and it was taking everything she had not to pull the trigger. For Sonya, for the city, for Prometheus. "Talk, pirate, like your life depends on it."

The man blinked. Blood gushed from his lip and down his chin. "I'm not a pirate."

Rance laughed.

"I'm not," he insisted, raising his hands. "The pirate symbols are a disguise."

"For who?" Solaris asked. His face had turned ashen.

"Nilurians."

Rance's mouth dropped open. They were Nilurian Rebels? How had they managed to organize this much force? Rance became even more incensed. Pirates polluting and pillaging was one thing, but a coordinated attack by an organization that claimed to devote itself to protecting the common man? An organization that led peaceful protests and fought for human rights?

Sonya had been a commoner. Who had protected her?

Rance holstered her blaster and drew her dagger. A clean death was too good for this one. The Rebel's eyes filled with horror as he realized what she was about to do.

Then, the fear left his eyes, and he crumpled to the ground. Rance gaped in surprise and looked around.

Solaris was standing quietly at her side, having just delivered a well-placed blow to the Rebel's head. Without killing him.

He fixed Rance with a shrewd gaze, but it wasn't accusing. "He's not worth it, Captain. Shouldn't we go?"

The street beyond the alley was filling with people. Slowly, Rance's head began to clear, and she could feel again. She felt mostly pain, and the traces of her anger faded into weariness. There was no time to contemplate what she'd almost done. They had to get back to the ship before it was overrun.

Where was James?

As if he'd heard his name, James appeared from somewhere behind, out of breath and looking relieved. He had a bag slung over his shoulder, stuffed full of something lumpy.

"There you are! Harper, you okay?"

Rance looked over at Harper, who was shaken but unharmed. Without waiting for any more disasters to befall them, the crew sprinted for the *Star Streaker*. As they exited the alley, a crowd was running for the ship. Some were closer than the crew was. They wouldn't make it in time. Rance almost stopped, sat down, and cried.

Just then, the ship took off, leaving a trail of street dust behind it.

"Tally's coming to get us!" James shouted.

Solaris looked like he wouldn't make another step. Rance put her arm under him to steady him.

"You might have to leave me," he whispered.

Rance snorted. "Don't be so dramatic, Sunshine. Nobody gets left behind when you're on my crew. How many times do I have to tell that thick skull of yours? I'm beginning to think I need to hit you over the head with your own staff."

"Don't. I'm too tired to block you."

The *Streaker* whined overhead. The crowd changed direction, following. As soon as the ship got close, Tally lowered the ramp. The blast from the engines threatened to knock them all off their feet.

First, James jumped up. Then Abel, pulling Harper with him.

James paused, a horrified look crossing his features. Rance turned, expecting the mob to be on top of them.

Instead, they were scattering. Some still sprinted for the

ship. Others were screaming and running in haphazard directions.

At the center was a gray-backed wolf-like creature with a spike on its tail. The same one that had chased them in the alley. As if seeking revenge, or attempting to flee the pirates itself, it turned toward the ship.

"*Go go go!*" Rance yelled.

Abel and James pulled Rance and Solaris into the ship. As soon as their feet hit the floor, the ramp closed. Rance caught a glimpse of fangs and saw the whites of the eyes of the people they were leaving behind. She didn't know whether to thank the creature for scattering the mob or to hope somebody killed it.

Then, the ship was maneuvering through the city, and the crew scrambled to buckle in for their escape.

———————

CHAPTER ELEVEN

W HEN R ANCE PULLED herself into the cockpit, she barely made it to her chair before her legs gave out. Solaris dragged himself up after her.

"You should go lie down," she said.

"No, thanks, I'd rather see my death coming."

He sat down but didn't bother to buckle in, propping his staff against his chair and hugging it. Despite what he'd just said about being able to see, he closed his eyes.

"Hey, *no one* is dying today," James said.

If only that were true, Rance thought. But James didn't know about their loss. The *Star Streaker* lifted off. Just as it cleared the buildings, a huge fireball hit the exact spot where they'd been sitting. The massive shock wave hit the *Streaker,* knocking it off course with a shudder. Rance bit her tongue, and the warm taste of iron filled her mouth.

"Triton's toes! They missed!" James said.

A small B-class fighter zoomed overhead, its dark green

hull looking out of place next to the black ships they had seen earlier.

Rance's heart raced in her chest, and blood rushed to her ears. But her body sagged into her chair, unable to process her fear fully. She stared out the window as if through someone else's eyes. Searing pain shot through her arm—a deep gash was bleeding freely. One of the rebels must have nicked Rance with his knife. She hadn't even realized it at the time. She covered the cut with her hand to avoid bleeding all over her seat.

"I think, Captain," James said, "that it's time for my stupidly stupid, death-defying trick."

"What's that?" Her words slurred. She must have been in worse shape than she thought.

"An in-atmosphere jump to hyperspace."

"James Fletcher, don't you dare!" Tally called over the comm.

Rance leaned over and switched it off. Then she addressed James.

"You'll have to jump like you did on Doxor 5—short and sweet. Then we'll prepare coordinates for a longer jump after we find an opening in the blockade."

"That means we'll have a short time where we'll be sitting in space like idiots, waiting for the Nilurians to paint a target on us."

"We don't have a choice." Rance flicked on the comm again. "Harper, tell Deliverance I need two sets of coordinates, to be used one right after the other."

"Yes, Captain."

"Is it wise to use Deliverance, Captain?" James asked. "After her malfunction?"

"We can't afford to get this wrong. Harper will double check her calculations."

Two small fighters appeared out of the sea of buildings, arcing gracefully between towers. They fired on the *Star Streaker* the second they came within range. James dipped and weaved back through the buildings, using the towers as cover.

"And hurry," Rance added to Harper.

Orange fireballs shot past, narrowly missing the *Streaker* and striking a glass building. A section of glass wall shattered, sending a shimmering, glittering rain of shards to the street below.

"That was close!" James said. "Where'd they come from?"

Rance studied the *Streaker's* sensors, which weren't meant for tracking enemy ships in a battle. But she saw two little dots blipping in and out between buildings behind them. "They're from those two small fighters, but you've lost them again."

Solaris sat with his chin on his chest—frowning, breathing, listening. Was he meditating? Rance didn't have time to ask before another rain of glass and fire fell from above, striking the shields and making Rance jump in her seat.

They were lucky the two fighters on their tail weren't equipped with guided missiles.

"Harper?" she asked.

"Almost there, Captain. Deliverance isn't cooperating."

"How so, Deliverance?"

To jump into hyperspace in such proximity to a planet and ships is unheard of, Captain. The likelihood of death is three trillion to one. I cannot participate in these calculations. Suggest surrender.

"The likelihood of death is much higher if we don't get out of here! We won't surrender, Deliverance."

"Captain," Harper interrupted, "we don't want to get this wrong. If the first jump is off by even a fraction of a degree, the second jump will send us into a part of space only the dead can find."

"Just get us there, Harper. Deliverance, *help her!*"

A silent pause. The crew held their breaths. The *Star Streaker* dipped down and flew into a narrow side street. Its wings were so close to the wall Rance imagined them leaving sparks. But James' experienced hands held the ship steady, waiting.

"Got them," Harper said. "Sending to you now."

The coordinates displayed on Rance's and James' displays.

"Everybody hold on," Rance said. "Good luck, James."

James scoffed, as if luck had nothing to do with it, and brought the *Streaker* out of the alleys. He maneuvered around another skyscraper, tilting the ship straight up for the clear sky ahead.

The hyperdrive spun up, sending vibrations throughout the ship. Rance could taste victory. They were going to make it.

Then, gliding over the city like a horrendous metal monster, a Renegade appeared above them.

Right in their jump path, pointing their cannons directly at the *Streaker*.

"Stop! James!" Rance yelled. Solaris opened his eyes and sat up, wide-eyed.

James was already correcting, punching a button and canceling the jump just in time. A collision alarm sounded. Rance punched it off as James banked left, away from the Renegade. More fighters zoomed around the buildings.

Rance held her breath, gripped her seat. There was nothing more she could do. No fancy tricks, no words of encouragement. Either James could out-fly them, or he couldn't. Their lives were in his hands.

More fire from the ships behind, but James had changed course before it pummeled their shields again. Instead, he flew straight at the slow-maneuvering Renegade. Alarms went off everywhere—collision alarms, weapons alarms.

"Shut them all down, Deliverance!" Rance yelled. The alarms shut off, leaving her ears ringing.

Even this close, the Renegade could fire a missile, hit the *Star Streaker,* and absorb any damage to its own hull. But the *Streaker* wouldn't survive. A direct hit would burst the *Streaker* and its crew into a thousand tiny pieces that would rain down on Prometheus like the glass from those buildings.

The ship shuddered again. Rance wasn't buckled in, and she held on tight so she wouldn't be thrown forward into James. Her broken fingers ached, but she forced herself to keep holding on.

"Something hit us," James said. "Shields still holding."

He zigzagged up, up, up. The Renegade couldn't turn fast enough, and soon the haze of the atmosphere faded, just as the first rays of dawn appeared on the horizon. Rance couldn't find the two fighters that had been pursuing, but she doubted they'd lost track of their prey. The blackness of space was before them.

And so were a hundred other ships. Of all makes and

models. Now that Rance knew they were facing organized rebels instead of individual clans of pirates, the game had become much more serious. Many of the Nilurian Rebels were ex-Unity.

And all of them would know about the tiny space cruiser trying to get off Prometheus.

"We'll never get past them," she whispered.

"Yes, we will," Solaris said. His voice cracked, but when he stood, he held himself confidently. As he lifted his staff, Rance scrambled to fasten her harness. Her aching fingers wouldn't work correctly, and she fumbled to snap the two halves together.

The fastener clicked in place, and then the *Star Streaker* rolled, pitching her to the right. As before, Solaris stood with his feet planted firmly on the floor of the cockpit. And while the ship rolled around and around, Rance felt the tug of centripetal force, like all the gravity on the ship had centered on Solaris.

With a jolt, she realized that was exactly what was happening.

Solaris was controlling gravity.

It wasn't without cost. His face drained of all color, and Rance thought he would kill himself for sure this time.

But she wasn't going to allow him to sacrifice himself for them. No one else would die today. "Solaris! STOP!"

Still, he held on, his eyes closed, his face becoming more haggard. His disguised face flickered like a bad video connection. For a second, Rance caught a glimpse of another face. But in the chaos, she couldn't make out any details.

The hyperdrive spun up of its own accord. James yelled that he couldn't control it.

Rance had to do something. They were out of control. And she couldn't lose another CO. Not like this. So, she did the most outrageous, most stupid thing she could think of.

She grabbed the handle that unfastened her harness and pulled.

It gave way, and she flew out of the seat, reaching out to tackle Solaris on her way. She collided with him, half-expecting his feet to be glued to the floor. But they weren't. His concentration broke, and he fell with her.

They crashed into a control panel behind Solaris' seat and landed in a heap on the floor. Rance grabbed him to keep from falling down the open hatch. The *Star Streaker* stopped spinning. The hyperdrive hummed as usual, ready for a command.

"We're clear!" James called. Rance looked up in time to see the last dark ship slide by. Then James gave the command, and the bright blue flash of hyperspace washed over the ship.

Solaris groaned. Rance pulled herself off him. She'd landed on his staff, which had tried to jab a hole in her ribs, creating a new wave of pain when she moved. But they were both alive, and she considered the move a success.

Solaris winced as she moved away. Harper climbed into the cockpit to see if she could assist.

"I'm sorry for leaving the ship, Captain," she said, blushing.

"Galley and lav duty for a month, Harper, but I'll consider waving it if you get everybody patched up."

"It's going to be a big job," she whispered as Solaris eased into a sitting position.

"Yes, it is," he replied.

CHAPTER TWELVE

"We've got to let people know what's happening on Prometheus," Rance said later.

They'd been in hyperspace thirty-six hours. The crew sat around the galley in varying states of exhaustion and wellness. Tally and James sat on either side of Rance. Neither had spoken to the other since the daring jump to hyperspace. It was just as well—Rance couldn't have dealt with any shouting.

Solaris sat with his head in his hands, breathing deeply. He might have been asleep. Although Rance burned with questions about how he had saved the *Star Streaker* and everybody in it, she didn't have the energy—or the heart—to question him about it right now. The promised answers would have to wait.

Abel sat at the other end of the bench and leaned on the wall. His face looked as bad as Solaris'—big purple bruises ringed his eye and cheek. Harper had offered to heal it for him in the med bay, but he'd refused, saying he'd wear it as a "badge of honor."

Rance didn't have any such notions of honor. She'd let Harper put her through several painful procedures to fix two cracked ribs, a broken finger, and bruising over eighty percent of her body. After, she felt better. Now, all injuries were on the mend, but she still felt like the *Star Streaker* had landed on top of her. Her head, which had been bashed around inside her helmet like a pebble inside an engine, throbbed when she moved it.

She didn't move it.

Henry had curled up into her lap and was emitting soft whistling noises and keeping her hands warm like a muff. Three days ago, the sounds would have been annoying. Today, they were oddly comforting.

Tania leaned against the wall near the table, behind Abel. She looked about to collapse but had refused to lay down or sleep much since they'd escaped. Rance could only imagine what was going through Tania's mind, but since her own thoughts were of Sonya, she guessed Tania's were too.

Moira rested in the med bay. She'd been injured as much as any of them, but she was also dealing with the weight of her actions on Prometheus. She'd wished to be alone.

The bag James had been carrying contained scavenged provisions. He had run across them in his search for Harper and gathered what he could on short notice. Now they were rationing what was left of it. But at least no one was going hungry.

Tally took a sip of Harper's tea. "How do you propose to let them know what's happening on Prometheus? Fly up to the nearest Unity ship and tell them?"

"Of course not. We can send a message somewhere."

"To whom? Who is going to trust an anonymous message from a star cruiser about a rebel attack on Prometheus?"

Rance took a deep breath and then winced. That still hurt. "Davos would believe me."

"You want to involve your *father*?" James asked, his eyebrows going up into his shaggy hair. "Harper, I think the Captain hit her head harder than you thought."

"I don't *want* to involve my father, but I think he would trust a message from me and see that it got to the right people."

"How can you be so sure?" James asked.

"The captain is correct," Tally said. "Lord Davos would believe it enough to send someone to check it out. But Captain, do you want to risk him being able to trace you?"

"I think it's worth the risk, Tally, don't you?"

Tally fixed his protruding green eyes on Rance. "Of course I do," he murmured.

"Then it's settled. How many hours left in hyperspace?" she asked James.

Deliverance responded before James could. *Two hours, Captain.*

Good. They wouldn't have to waste any more time.

"Deliverance, I need a good waystation in which to send a message to Xanthes. We'll only be there long enough to send the message from one of their beacons and find some food. Then we'll leave again."

"We'll still be traced, Captain," Solaris said, raising his head.

His eyes were red-rimmed and puffy. Had he been crying? Or was that the effect of Henry? A long trail of white skin glue ran down from his forehead to his cheek. Harper had said it wouldn't scar. Since Solaris could change his face, Rance wondered if they'd ever know if it did, anyway. A sudden, intense desire to see his real face almost caused her to miss what he was saying.

"...once Unity gets wind that the same ship that fled Doxor 5 is sending messages to Lord Davos, they'll swarm every known waystation in the empire. Is that an acceptable risk?"

Losing the ability to use the waystations would hamper future smuggling jobs, but they could manage it. "I think so, yes," she said.

Solaris stood—carefully—and climbed off the bench. "I'll go prepare a message."

"You'll do no such thing," Rance said. "I'll record the message. I won't leave anything to chance."

She climbed off the bench ever so slowly, wondering if she would even be able to get up the ladder and into the cockpit without help.

"Want me to go with you, Captain?" James asked.

Rance paused. She really needed the help, but contacting her father was a private matter. A few days ago, she'd told Solaris she didn't have any secrets from the crew—and she didn't—but she hadn't spoken to Davos since she ran away from home, more than five years ago. The message would be personal, and she'd likely have to record it several times before she was satisfied.

"No, James. I can manage."

"Very good, Captain," James said, turning back to his own tea and smirking. "You look like you're managing quite well.

I'll just listen for any sounds of distress, and then pointedly ignore them, since they won't be from you."

Rance shot him a dirty look and left the galley.

The walk to the cockpit was the longest trip of Rance's life. She paused on the second step of the stairway, wincing when she discovered new pain in places she didn't know she had. She would have glanced back to make sure no one was looking, but moving her head was dicey. So, she gathered what pride she had left and continued, pausing every couple of steps.

The conversation in the galley drifted out to her.

"Why are Nilurian Rebels attacking Prometheus?" James asked.

"Easy," Abel said. "They're trying to start a war."

"Don't call them rebels," Solaris said with more vehemence than Rance would have thought possible. "They attacked a Core world, killed innocent people. They're no better than the pirates they stole the standard from."

Finally, Rance reached the top deck, and their voices faded. From there, walking was easy compared to climbing stairs. She gave a longing look into her quarters and her too-short but comfortable bed. But she passed them and made her way down the corridor.

At the end of the deck, Rance stared at the cockpit ladder a full ten minutes before summoning the energy to put her foot on the bottom rung. Climbing up into the cockpit took longer than she cared to admit, but when she finally emerged, she breathed a sigh of relief and eased into her chair. The blue wash of hyperspace blocked out the stars, but it bathed the cockpit in a soothing, pleasant glow. Good thing, too, because she might be forced to stay there until her body healed, or someone took pity on her and moved her below deck.

"Deliverance, prepare a video transmission."

The next moment, the screen in front of her showed Rance's face. Rance took a deep breath. She could record the message as many times as she needed. No need to be nervous.

Her underarms were sweaty, her palms clammy. She refused to attribute her nervousness to her task. Just because she was going to talk to her father for the first time in five years didn't mean she was a little girl again.

No. Like Solaris said, Rance was a changed woman. Davos might not even recognize her. Part of her wished he would. Part of her hoped he wouldn't. Since the success of this message depended on him recognizing her, though, she settled for the former.

Finally, Rance stopped thinking about it and spoke to the screen.

"Record."

A red light blinked in the top corner. It was ready.

She took a deep breath, sat up tall, and said, "Hello, Father."

EPILOGUE

LORD DAVOS SAT behind his desk in his dark office, brooding out the expansive window onto the nighttime city below. A dust storm was brewing. In the distance, lightning streaked across the clouds, illuminating swirling eddies of purple sand. The smell of the poisonous chirkwood flower potted in the corner tickled his nose. He was tempted to throw it out the window. Tonight, everything offended him—the city, the planet Xanthes, his failure to control the actions of his family.

He'd just watched Devri's message. His daughter—his *only* daughter—had just fled a planet full of pirates. She'd endangered herself again—more proof that she was incapable of commanding her own starship. As if Davos needed more proof. Lately, tales of her exploits had reached him with alarming frequency. He always heard of them too late to catch her. Some idiot bungled the reporting or didn't recognize her in time. Each report caused Davos' anger to surge higher.

And now, pirates.

Davos scoffed. No, not pirates, *rebels*. His distaste for the Nilurian Rebels ran deeper than for the pirates. Pirates only wanted to be left to their own devices. For the most part, they managed themselves and occasionally benefitted the empire with their illegal trade. When they got too big and too cocky, the empire cut them down.

But *rebels*. Davos despised their misguided ideology, their self-appointed missions for the common man. If the Nilurians had their way, the empire would descend into anarchy. And then who would keep the pirates at bay?

No, Triton would cut down the rebels too. If they had dared to attack a Core world, it was time for the Empire Triton to show them why Unity's forces were so good at keeping the alien worlds in check.

Davos took a swig from his flask, the one carrying his special concoction that included poison from the plant in the corner. It no longer burned when it went down, but still left a metallic, bitter taste on his tongue.

Or was it the bitterness left by his missing wife, Jane? He hadn't heard from her in over a year. After she and Devri had left five years ago, he'd only received curt transmissions from her. And even those had stopped. He didn't think she was in danger. Probably living it up at society balls on Coru or Triton. She always did care more about mingling with the nobility on those worlds than the ones on Xanthes.

Hopefully, she hadn't been on Prometheus when it was attacked. Davos sat down the flask with a heavy clink, stirring himself to his work. It wasn't in his nature to ask *what if*, only to deal with the problems at hand. He sent secure transmissions to Emperor Arthos, detailing what he knew about the attack on Prometheus. Arthos had been too long-suffering with the rebels. And they had repaid him with treason.

Davos sniffed derisively. Let the emperor deal with the problem he'd created.

For Davos, the need to find his daughter had grown more pressing than ever. The last thing he wanted was for her to get killed, caught in some scuffle between the empire and the rebels. If only he knew what her ship looked like, he could retrieve her. So far, he'd had trouble pinning down its registration or getting accurate accounts of its physical appearance. Everyone who'd encountered her recently—and he'd spoken to each one of them—said her ship kept changing midflight. Like she was hopping from ship to ship to confuse her pursuers. How she'd managed that trick, he wasn't sure.

With his blood pressure rising and the rock in his stomach growing heavier, Davos pulled out his handset to comm a servant. Before he could make a request, however, his comm beeped. Lord Aron.

Davos answered with a terse, "What?"

"Lord Davos, I trust I find you well?"

His wheedling voice grated on Davos' nerves at the best of times. It sounded even worse over the comm. Davos was in no mood for pleasantries, especially from Francivi Aron.

"What is it, Aron?"

"I have some news of your daughter."

Davos sat up and leaned over the comm. "Yes?"

"A Lieutenant Arnold contacted the Unity base, saying he ran into Devri a week ago."

"And *did he bring her back with him?*" Davos snarled.

"No, my lord. I'm afraid not."

Of course, he hadn't. If he had, Devri would already be home. "Why am I not surprised? Tell me, Aron, is there any competent officer left in Unity? Or have they all defected to the pirates and rebel sympathizers?"

Maybe the reason the rebels had swept into Prometheus like they had was because all the bright ones had sought out greener pastures. Davos brought a fist down on the desk. "Answer me!"

Aron hesitated, but when he spoke, he seemed nonplussed by Davos' impatience.

"He was confused. He didn't realize who he had until it was too late."

"Then he is as useless as you. Why did he even bother to report?"

"Because," Aron said, ignoring the insult, "he knows what Devri's ship looks like."

Davos sat back, digesting the information. "Are you sure?"

"Lieutenant Arnold is sure."

"I want to speak with him personally."

"Of course, my lord."

"Send him now, before he has an accident and forgets."

Davos clicked off the comm and stood to pace in front of the window. If he had a description of the ship, he could pull security footage from the waystations. Devri had used one of them to send her message. He knew which one, of course, but it was a busy location, and thousands of ships used it every day. But if they knew what her ship looked like, they could find out what time she arrived, what time she left, and if they were lucky, her destination.

Davos commed Lord Aron again.

"Yes?"

"On your way here, stop and pick up McConnell."

"I'm assuming you mean the younger McConnell, Harrison, and not his esteemed father."

"Yes," Davos grumbled. "It's time that man earned some of his inheritance, instead of wasting it at the tavern."

It took more than two hours for Aron to arrive with Arnold and McConnell in tow. While Davos waited, he had sent more messages, demanding security footage, arrivals, and departures from the waystation. In between calls, he fumed. The house servants had avoided his office like he had a case of arlakan plague. And when they escorted Aron and his charges to Davos' office, they held back at the door.

Davos waved the servants away.

Lord Francivi Aron looked conniving as ever, with his crooked-tooth smile and his thin, pallid face. Lieutenant Arnold was brown-skinned and young. Probably close to Devri's age. He looked nervous, but he saluted Davos and stood up straight, waiting to be addressed.

Harrison McConnell looked like he'd just been dragged from under a table. His robes were dirty and crumpled, his face red. But he stood as still as he could manage. Aron must have put the fear of Triton into him to get him to sober up on the way over.

Without standing on ceremony, Davos nodded at Arnold, signaling him to begin his tale. The young man cleared his throat and tried not to stare at anything in particular as he recounted his run-in with Devri and her crew. The details about the encounter were fuzzier than Davos would have liked, but Arnold gave vivid descriptions of the crew members and the ship which had been called the *Stanley Alto*.

McConnell snorted.

"Something funny?" Davos sneered. The man really was an idiot. Davos could see why Devri despised him. It was a shame he belonged to the most influential family on Xanthes.

McConnell glanced at Aron and then shook his head. "No, sir."

Always one to detect a lie, Davos stalked over to McConnell and stared him down. "You don't think Devri is on that ship?"

"Oh, umm. Yes, sir, I do think she is."

The younger man's eyes shifted slightly. The ZOD in Davos' eye registered an elevated heart rate. McConnell was hiding something.

"Do you know something I don't?"

"No, sir." He returned Davos' gaze without wavering.

Davos' mouth drew into a thin, hard line. He would have taken the opportunity to threaten McConnell, but Lieutenant Arnold was looking distinctly uncomfortable. Davos didn't care about the fool's discomfort, but he didn't want him telling people that Davos threatened his future son-in-law, either.

"Lieutenant," he said, still staring at McConnell, "tell me what happened after you boarded the ship."

"Ah. That's when things get a bit confusing, sir."

"Did you see my daughter or not?"

"Yes, sir. I'm certain I did."

Davos walked over to Arnold. "Is there something to make you doubt it?"

"Once I got onboard, I spoke to her. She recognized me— we went to the Xanthes Flight Academy together."

"Did you?" Davos scowled. Sending her to that Academy and indulging her whims had been one of his biggest mistakes.

"Yes, sir. And I remember putting her in energy cuffs."

"You *what?*" Davos fumed. "You imbecile. How dare you put a noblewoman in cuffs without direct written orders!"

Arnold winced and said weakly, "I'm sorry, sir."

Davos had long ago lost his patience. The lieutenant was lucky that he made it a policy not to strike Unity officers. But he was sorely tempted.

"And then what happened?" he ground out through his teeth.

"And then—" Arnold glanced at Aron, as if for help. But Lord Aron eyes were as cold as ice—he wasn't going to bail him out. Arnold's voice grew to a whisper. "I lost her. I led her to the stairs where her crew was. Her CO told me to unlock the cuffs, and I did."

Davos roared, wishing he had something in his hand to chuck at the lieutenant. He really wanted to throttle him.

Aron, seeing Davos ready to burst a vein, intervened. "And then I suppose you just went back to your own ship and flew away?"

"Yes, sir."

McConnell snorted again, close to laughter. All three stared at him as if he'd come unhinged.

"Out with it, McConnell," Aron said.

McConnell snickered again and held up his hand in apology. "My lords, did you expect anything less from Devri?"

"Not *less*," Davos said, glaring at Arnold. "But I do expect Unity officers not to lose their heads when she smiles at them."

"Sir!" Arnold said, stung. "It wasn't like that. Something happened on that ship. I don't know. One minute, I was in control of everything, and the next, I couldn't remember where I was or why I had her in cuffs."

"Are you sure she didn't knock you over the head for using cuffs on her?" McConnell asked.

Arnold turned red. "I'm glad you find this so amusing."

"Oh, I do. I really do. None of you"—he looked pointedly at Davos—"in here know anything about Devri."

"I went to school with her!"

"And yet you didn't know her well enough to anticipate a double-cross."

Davos snarled. "Watch your mouth, McConnell. Are you suggesting Devri is duplicitous?"

"No, sir, only resourceful."

Davos loomed over McConnell. "And you think you can be just as resourceful?"

"I didn't say that."

"But you are implying it." Davos glared at him out of habit, but he was thinking. If McConnell claimed to know his daughter better than her own father, maybe he should send the man out to get her. He was a bungling, greedy idiot, but at least it would get McConnell out of the way for a while. And maybe he'd make a fool of himself somewhere other than the taverns on Xanthes. Yes, it was a good idea. Davos jabbed a finger into McConnell's face. "Pack a bag."

McConnell paled. "Sir?"

"You have just become the new head of the search for Devri. If you know her as well as you claim, finding her and her ship shouldn't be a problem. I don't know why I didn't think of it before. If you want to marry her, you'll go out and get her."

McConnell sputtered. "But sir, I wouldn't know where to begin."

"We have a description of the ship. I'm having security videos sent as we speak." Davos jerked his head toward Arnold. "And the lieutenant here will escort you wherever you need to go."

"I will?"

"If you don't want to be stripped of your rank and thrown in with the enlisted, then yes, you will. You will ferry McConnell and find my daughter." Davos glared at them. "And make sure my future son-in-law doesn't get distracted by anything along the way."

McConnell and Arnold both gaped at Davos. Arnold, who had too much to lose if he didn't comply, pulled himself together and saluted. McConnell, however, looked like he would argue.

Seeing McConnell wavering, Lord Aron cleared his throat. "I'm sure Harrison would love to bring his future bride back to Xanthes."

McConnell glanced at Aron, looking defeated.

Still feeling like they were keeping something from him, Davos narrowed his eyes. "It should be an honor, McConnell. You still want to marry my daughter, correct?"

His tone dared McConnell to say something in disagreement. Like Devri, McConnell didn't have a choice in the matter, but Davos would sooner betray the Emperor than let

McConnell admit he didn't want to go through with the marriage.

McConnell tore his eyes away from Lord Aron to look at Davos. "Of course I do, sir. The honor will be all mine."

"Good. We don't have a minute to lose. You leave tonight."

A CONVERSATION

BONUS SHORT STORY

A WEEK AFTER LEAVING PROMETHEUS, life aboard the *Star Streaker* had improved. Rance had sent a message to her father from Waystation 10, a space station between Prometheus and the Nilurian Belt. It handled millions of transmissions a day from thousands of ships, the perfect place to send an anonymous message. As soon as he received it, her father would have tried to trace her. But with all the traffic, spotting Rance on security footage would have been difficult.

Communicating with Davos at all was risky. In the five years Rance had been captain of the *Star Streaker*, she'd never been tempted to contact him. But she and the crew agreed that the attack on Prometheus was bigger than Rance's issues with her father or the threat of an arranged marriage.

Her biggest worry was that Davos had a description of her ship, but it had been a risk she was willing to take.

The risk had paid off. A day after she sent the message, Unity ships descended on the Nilurian Rebels besieging the planet. Either Davos had received Rance's message, or a separate call for help had gotten through the rebels' blockade. A terrifying battle had ensued. But after two days of intense fighting and bitter losses on both sides, the rebels fled the planet.

Prometheus was in ruins. Whole cities had been destroyed. Millions of people had been displaced.

And no one knew why. If the Nilurians had intended to start a war, they had given up quickly. Unity was currently pursuing the scattered remnants of the rebel fleet across the empire.

A happy consequence meant that Unity would no longer actively hunt for Rance and Solaris. It wasn't the way she wanted, but she was grateful for a reprieve from being chased everywhere she went.

While at Waystation 10, Rance contracted to courier a shipment of completely ordinary, harmless neural circuits for a small armorer. The circuits were used in heads-up displays for custom helmets. The most out-of-the-ordinary thing about them was that they were legal. Rance triple-checked the company's credentials before agreeing to transport them. She didn't want any more trouble, nor was she keen to endanger her crew's lives again.

Ever.

Two days after taking on their cargo, Rance walked the ship on night patrol. She padded through the peaceful ship in her bare feet. The ice-cold metal floor bit into her skin, but it felt good, kept her alert. Being in her bare feet wouldn't be prudent if they ran into trouble, but Rance's broken toe, although healed, still ached when she crammed it into boots. Her other injuries were in varying states of healing, but she could walk and move around without much discomfort.

Always having someone on duty didn't use to matter much in hyperspace. Unless the *Star Streaker* was going to be sucked into a black hole, they had been safe in their little dimensional time bubble. But ever since Solaris had told her that the empire had ships that could follow another ship into hyperspace, Rance had insisted someone be on duty continuously.

She walked into the galley, intent on finding a midnight snack. Since Solaris had gone to bed hours before, she was surprised to see him sitting at the table, eating a piece of double chocolate cake. Beside him, his handset sat on the table, projecting a holographic, 3D puzzle into the air. He swiped lazily at a puzzle piece, assembling a monochromatic image that looked like an ancient sailboat on the water.

After weeks of tightening their belts, the crew could finally afford to feed themselves. Moira had paid Rance handsomely for getting her off Prometheus. After the loss of Sonya, Rance hadn't wanted to take the money. It didn't seem right to profit from so much loss. She would have gone to Prometheus even if they had known about the pirates ahead of time.

Rebels, not pirates, she reminded herself.

But Tally had pointed out that if Rance didn't take the money, their days of flying from system to system would be over. And the crew needed to be paid, the *Star Streaker* repaired. It had received some minor damage to the hull during their flight, but also several circuits boards had needed replacing after Deliverance shorted them out.

Rance grabbed a clean fork from a drawer and leaned across the table to steal a bite of Solaris' cake. Chocolate wasn't her favorite, but she figured her body was still healing from all its injuries, and she needed the extra fuel.

"Did you learn to steal cake at your father's dinner parties?" Solaris asked without looking up from his puzzle. His face had almost healed, his humor somewhat returned. He'd been more quiet than usual, though. They all had.

The cake was better than Rance had expected. She sat down across from him and smiled ruefully. "Davos' chef used to make cakes so tall they reached the ceiling of the solarium. Or they mimicked the purple fountains in the courtyard, with icing that looked like flowing water."

"You lived such a hard life out on Xanthes."

"It had its challenges. Ever been to a nobleman's party?"

"Once, on Triton."

Rance raised an eyebrow in surprise. "Really."

"Lots of fake hair, copious amounts of makeup, and more scheming than a cave fox in a hen house."

"What were you doing at a party on Triton?"

"Chasing down an interplanetary assassin."

"You're just making that up."

Solaris swiped the final piece of his puzzle into place and then looked up. "I'm not. Former Galaxy Wizard, remember?"

"So, tell me about that."

"The assassin?"

"Being a Galaxy Wizard."

"As I told you a few days ago, those aren't things I can talk about."

Rance rolled her eyes. "Just talk about it in general. I'm not looking for imperial secrets. Do you miss it?"

Solaris sat back, regarding her. "Do you miss being a nobleman's daughter?"

Rance shook her head. "No."

"Well then." Solaris looked back at his cake as if he'd just answered her question.

"But you're thinking of going back," she said, realization taking hold. The idea made her stomach queasy, although she didn't want to think about why.

"If rebels are openly attacking Core worlds, the Wizards will need everyone they can get."

"Will they accept you back? I thought you were a wanted man."

"I am. And I haven't changed my mind about their new methods. But under extenuating circumstances, they might grant clemency so I can work for them again. There aren't enough Galaxy Wizards anyway."

"Why not?"

"Recruitment is low. They handpick people. Orphans, mostly."

Rance remembered what Solaris had told her that night at Moira's, while they watched Prometheus burn, about losing his family when he was very young. "Orphans like you?"

He nodded. "Like me."

"Do you think of yourself as an orphan?"

"Nah." He smiled. "I have you, Captain," he said, then added as an afterthought, "...and the crew. Before that, I had the other Wizards. They were my family."

"I imagine they are holding a grudge since you left."

"You could say that."

Rance eyed the rest of his cake. She was burning with

questions. Her curiosity had intensified ever since they'd left Prometheus, but she'd never found the opportunity to question him. Until now. "What did you do to become the most wanted man in the Galaxy?"

Solaris smirked. "Thought you didn't like chocolate."

"This chocolate is okay."

"Why?"

"Because it had already been dished out. I was feeling too lazy to fix myself something." Rance stole another bite and winked at him.

Solaris looked at her warmly. "Are you flirting, Rance Cooper?"

Rance turned as red as their pet cappatter's fur and choked on her cake. She sputtered for an embarrassing length of time, in which Solaris got her a cup of water and stood at the ready, possibly to do the Heimlich maneuver.

When Rance managed to breathe again, she waved him off. "I'm not going to die."

"Good. It would be unfortunate if your dying breath were used to flirt with *me*."

Rance took a sip of the water and washed down the burning in her throat. "I only wanted your cake, not to flirt with you."

Solaris sat down across the table and laughed, his first in days. "You could have asked."

Then, he pushed the rest of it over to her.

Rance smiled at the gesture, but she wasn't sure she wanted anymore after she'd nearly asphyxiated on the last bite.

"So?" she asked. "Why do the Galaxy Wizards want you so badly?"

"It's complicated."

Rance waited for Solaris to begin the story. But he didn't. Instead, he busied himself with turning the holographic puzzle around and around on its axis.

"I don't have those portentous dreams much anymore," he whispered after a moment.

Rance lowered her voice, too, although they were the only crew members awake. "The ones about the galaxy burning? Isn't that a good thing?"

Solaris met her eyes. Pain and regret crossed his face. His eyes had taken on a haunted look, one Rance was surprised to see on him.

He took a deep breath. "It makes me wonder if I left the Wizards for nothing. What if those dreams were just... dreams? Leftover nightmares from my childhood?"

"Then you left an organization you still didn't agree with. Isn't that the right thing?"

"Yes. And no. Not the way I left it."

When Solaris didn't elaborate, Rance toyed with pressing him for more information, but she couldn't bring herself to do it. Whatever the reason, Solaris was haunted by something. If he wanted to share, he would.

To steer the conversation toward a more innocuous topic, Rance asked, "How did you meet Harrison McConnell, then? Please tell me he wasn't the assassin."

Solaris snorted. "I thought you knew him?"

"I do—I'm still *technically* betrothed to him."

"Then you know that Harrison couldn't assassinate anybody if they laid down at his feet and did it for him."

Rance laughed. "So how did *you* meet him?"

"By chance. After leaving the Wizards, I hitched a ride

to Xanthes to look for work, and for a lowly position on a ship where I could stay under the radar. Harrison was at the spaceport one day while I was asking around. His father runs it, apparently." Solaris looked to Rance for confirmation.

She nodded. "That and ten others across Xanthes."

"And yet you don't want to marry Harrison? Why not?" Solaris grinned mischievously.

Rance looked at the last bit of cake. Maybe it wouldn't kill her. She stuck her fork into it. "Like you said, I've met him. That's enough to deter anybody. So, then what happened?"

"I asked if he knew of anyone needing a crew member, showed him my credentials."

"Your *fake* credentials. You lied to me."

"I didn't. Everything I told you about me is true."

"You didn't go to the Xanthes Flight Academy."

"Not as a student, but I was there. Undercover as an officer."

"And the Renegade and Destroyers you served on?"

"Again, undercover."

Rance finished off the cake and looked at him. The haunted look had passed, and she was glad of her decision to direct the conversation elsewhere. She wasn't any less curious though.

"You do get around," she said. "It must be hard to stay happy on a small space cruiser when you can have all that undercover excitement."

"I don't know," Solaris said thoughtfully. "There's been quite enough excitement for me here. Before you hired me, did you always get into so much trouble? Or is that just something that happened after you had me around to get you out of jams?"

Rance scoffed. "I got out of plenty of tight spots before I met you. Which reminds me."

Solaris raised an eyebrow. "Yes?"

"What did you do to me on Prometheus? In the crowd." She didn't have to add that it was after they'd found out about Sonya's death. Solaris would know what she meant. Rance had been furious with the pirates. He had used some sort of trick to calm her down and probably saved her life. Attacking those pirates alone would have been suicide.

"Are you offended?" he asked.

"At first."

Solaris frowned. "And now?"

"No. I know you were only trying to help. But we've never talked about this."

"About what?"

"About the fact that you are the most powerful man I've ever met."

"Don't think about me that way. I'm the same as you."

"Yeah right."

"I am. Listen, Captain, I'd prefer you to think of me as an ordinary guy."

Rance leaned forward, placing her hands on the table. "Solaris, your powers are beyond comprehension. I could never beat you in a fight. And you're on board *my* ship, running loose."

Amusement flashed in his eyes. "Running loose? I'm not a pet who wreaks havoc. You already have one of those."

"It's not that."

"Then what? You're not afraid of me."

Rance shook her head. "No. I trust you, which is why I'm not offended that you did some mind-altering magic to keep me from making a mistake. But again, we've never talked about this."

Solaris took a deep breath and spread his arms out in an open gesture. "Okay. What do you want to talk about?"

"What will you tell me?"

"Anything I can. Just no specifics about assignments. I should have explained more before now, but we were all getting along..."

"We're *still* getting along. But you can't blame me for being curious. Before I met you, I thought the Galaxy Wizards were a myth."

"Where should I start?"

"If you're a wizard, why don't you wear a cloak?" Rance swished her arms out to her side, mimicking the movement of flowing fabric behind her.

Solaris snorted. "The cloak question again? Those went out of style centuries ago. And it's a bit hard to stay under-cover when wearing one. Also, they make you trip and fall on your face, as I think I've mentioned."

"Sounds like the voice of experience talking."

"The Wizards wear them for ceremonies only."

Rance imagined Solaris wearing a long, hooded cloak. It would make him look more imposing than he was. She wouldn't mind seeing him in one, just once.

"They really aren't that flattering," he said, perhaps guessing her thoughts.

Rance smirked and changed the subject. "How about your powers? What did you do to the *Streaker* when we left Prometheus?"

"That was especially difficult."

"You messed with gravity to get us away from those ships."

Solaris looked impressed. "Excellent!"

"So you *can* control gravity?"

"Not exactly. I can manipulate it to some degree."

"And how did that keep us from being blown to bits by those rebel ships?"

"I changed our pattern through space by manipulating the space-time around us."

"You're talking about a wormhole?" Rance was stunned. "You can create them?"

"It's more like I can bend space. But yes, it's something like a wormhole. And only for very short distances."

Rance gaped at him, her mouth hanging open in shock. Of course, modern science had studied wormholes at length, and before developing hyperspace, used them to colonize new parts of the galaxy. And Solaris could create one on his own?

Solaris reached across the table and put his hand under her chin, closing her mouth. "I've never known you to be speechless."

Again, his fingers felt smoother than they should have. She thought about when he'd taken her hand on Prometheus. She grabbed his hand before he could retract it, and turned it over, palm up.

It looked normal, had lines, some worn calluses. When she felt it, though, his skin was as smooth as a baby's, with some odd wrinkles. She ran her fingers over his palm, marveling at the difference between the way it looked and the way it felt.

"Are you going to hold my hand all night, Rance, or can I have it back sometime soon?"

But Rance didn't let go. Instead, she pointed to his palm. "Do you disguise your hands along with your face?"

"Yes," he answered matter-of-factly.

"Why are they so smooth?" Her eyes widened. "You're not a girl, are you?"

Solaris burst out laughing and slapped his other hand on the table. Tears of mirth sprang to his eyes. "No," he said between chortles. "All male. You don't want to see my real hands."

"Why not?"

Solaris sobered a bit. "Some ugly scarring. I prefer to keep it hidden."

"What happened?"

He seemed to debate something. Caught up in the moment, Rance realized she may have overstepped her boundaries. The question had been extremely personal. "I'm sorry, I—"

Solaris shook his head. "It's okay. It happened a long time ago. When the Wizards found me, I had severe burns from the fire that took the lives of my family."

"Oh." Rance felt like a heel. She shouldn't have asked. Realizing she was still holding his hand, she released it.

But Solaris didn't withdraw as if he were angry. He smiled. "The scars are nothing to look at really. Except for some reason, when people see me, they feel the need to stare. Even my fellow Wizards, when we were kids. I found them looking at the scars on my face and hands without looking at *me*, you know? That's why I learned to disguise myself so well. Orion taught me."

"I'm sorry," Rance said again.

"It's alright. It doesn't stop me from being the most powerful man you know." Solaris winked.

Rance squirmed in her seat. Solaris was only two years older than she, but his life had been drastically different from hers. What he had endured, what he had accomplished. The shape of his life seemed deeper, weightier, like it took up more space in the universe than hers ever could. He had made an impact on countless lives. Could Rance say the same?

Suddenly, she felt ashamed for complaining about an arranged marriage when the man sitting across from her had lost everything, gained it, and lost it again. Compared to his trials, hers seemed insignificant. Next to him, Rance felt... inadequate.

"Does it bother you to know?" Solaris asked, watching her.

"No," she answered truthfully. "But it bothers me that you thought it might bother me."

"It bothered me that I thought it might bother you, which is why I hesitated to bother you about it."

Rance shook her head in confusion. "What?"

He grinned.

She grinned back, shaking off the feeling of being on uneven ground. "Okay. Since it doesn't *bother* me, how bad are the burns?"

"Right side of my face, both hands, and the right half of my chest. Something burning fell on me, and I tried to push it off. At least that's what they tell me. I don't really remember it, except in dreams."

Solaris ran a hand through his sandy-colored hair. Rance wanted to ask him to show her his real face. But she hesitated.

He glanced at her and seemed to know what she was thinking.

"Maybe another time," he murmured. "It's been a long time since anyone has seen the real me."

"But I have seen the real you, Solaris," she said, feeling a surge of friendship for him.

He raised an eyebrow.

"You're a genuinely good person. You're kind and honorable, and you stick by your friends. That's all I really need to know."

"Ah." Solaris cleared his throat uncomfortably. "I wish you hadn't said that. It makes me feel like an imposter."

"What?" Rance could not imagine what caring, brave Solaris had done that would change her good opinion of him. She shook her head.

"Maybe we should leave it at that for tonight," he said, standing.

Realizing how tired she was, Rance stood too and made for the door. Solaris followed her out of the galley. On their way out, she waved her hand at a panel near the door, and the lights turned off. Rows of green, glowing lights outlined the cargo hold and followed the stairs to the top deck. They cast a faint glow over their faces.

"You can get some sleep, Captain. I'm awake."

Rance turned to Solaris. He was looking at her with the same warm expression he'd had earlier. She imagined how horrible it would be to hide her appearance because it made people uncomfortable. It didn't make her pity him, but she had a newfound appreciation for his inner strength.

"Solaris."

"Hmm?"

"Why do you get so tired after using your powers?" Rance refrained from calling it "magic" for now until she clarified that. Instead, she added it to the mental list that had grown, not shortened, since she'd walked into the galley a few minutes before.

"I'm not infallible."

"But why?"

Solaris sighed. "Because I haven't returned to the Temple Station. There, we recharge, so to speak. With regular visits, our powers are strengthened. It has something to do with the station itself. After being gone a while, my powers take longer to revive. *I* take longer to revive, especially after a particularly arduous task."

Rance gasped. "But what will happen if you never return? Will you lose your powers completely?"

"Maybe."

"But then you can't..." She trailed off, not wanting to offend him about his appearance.

"I can't change my face?" he asked, completing her question. "We'll see."

Solaris put his hand on the railing. The movement was subtle, but it brought him a little closer to Rance.

"Are you the first Galaxy Wizard to run away?" she asked.

"Others have left, or deserted, or turned traitor, but that was a long time ago."

"Did they keep their powers?"

"I don't know."

"Don't you think you should find out?"

Solaris rolled his eyes. "No, Rance, it never crossed my mind. Whatever would I do without your searing intellect?"

Rance narrowed her eyes. "If you keep rolling your eyes, they'll get stuck like that."

"Is that what happened to you?"

She swatted his arm.

Solaris laughed. "That's a great comeback. Did you just want an excuse to touch me?"

Rance's face warmed. Did he really think she was flirting with him? Was she?

No. She wasn't. She thought of Solaris like she thought of James—a brother or a friend.

As Rance turned to climb the stairs, she wondered why she was trying to convince herself. She had a firm policy against flirting with fellow crew members. After all, Solaris had said he might leave. A knot clenched in Rance's gut. Realizing she'd never addressed that possibility, she turned back.

Solaris still stood at the bottom of the stairs.

"Solaris."

"What now?" he asked, although there was no hint of exasperation in his voice, merely friendly banter. In the dark, she couldn't see his face at all anymore.

"If you go back to the Galaxy Wizards, I'll have to look for another CO."

"Yes, you will," he said seriously.

"Would you... would you consider staying? I'd hate to go through all that again."

"You can't seem to keep a CO, can you?"

"What's wrong with me?" she asked, feeling suddenly vulnerable.

"Nothing at all," he murmured. Then he added, "I suspect it has something to do with all the trouble you get into, but that doesn't account for the rest of your crew. They seem content to stay."

"And you're not?"

"I am. For now. I haven't decided to leave."

"Well, if you do, let me know in time to find a replacement."

Rance turned away and climbed the last two stairs. The suggestion that Solaris might leave hurt her heart. Replacing him wouldn't be easy. But she didn't want to accidentally betray her thoughts to him. After all, if he thought leaving would be best, who was she to stand in his way?

"Goodnight," he called up to her.

"Goodnight," she said.

Rance's foot brushed up against something soft.

Henry.

"Hello, fluffball," she whispered.

The furry ginger blob held out four arms to her, his blue eyes looking sleepy and happy all at the same time. Abel was supposed to keep the cappatter in a box at night, but apparently, it had learned to escape that too.

Rance smiled, remembering how the creature had reminded her of Solaris. She sighed in resignation, picked up Henry, and looked up and down the hall. After making sure no one was watching, she cuddled Henry close to her head. She hadn't forgotten he was the reason for her broken toe, but she had an overwhelming desire to hug something.

Henry nuzzled her, wrapping two skinny arms around her face. His soft fuzzy hair smelled like warm cinnamon, and he trilled contentedly. Rance carried him to her door.

"He's a cute little thing, isn't he, Captain?"

Startled, Rance spun around.

James had come out of his quarters and was leaning against the doorjamb. His look, even in the green glow of the lights, was triumphant and joyful.

"Don't you tell *anybody*," Rance whispered vehemently. "Or you'll be scrubbing the lav for the next month."

"We have automatic cleaning systems."

"I'll turn them off." Rance glared at him. But she didn't let go of Henry. She doubted she could, anyway. He had burrowed his arms into her hair.

James held up his hands and snorted. "Wouldn't dream of telling anyone, Captain."

And then he smiled.

ACKNOWLEDGMENTS

A big shout out to the Phoenix Prime crew for their support, advice, feedback, editing, and occasional kick in the pants. Without them, I would not have finished this book when I did. Or even started the *Star Streaker* series this year.

Special thanks to Ana and Carina for being awesome beta readers, and Jeanne for editing *Prometheus Rescue*. And thanks to Ana for beta reading and Diane for editing "A Conversation." You are awesome, and I don't know what I would do without you.

As always, a huge thank you to my hubby, Eric, who puts up with me disappearing for long hours to get my writing done. He's been my biggest supporter throughout this journey. I love you, baby!

ABOUT THE AUTHOR

T.M. (Tiffany) Catron spent her childhood looking for hidden worlds in the back of her closet. When she didn't find any, she decided to grow up already and write them into existence.

She's the author of the post-apocalyptic sci-fi series, *Shadowmark*, and the space opera (with wizards!) series, *Star Streaker*. Her stories tend to include strong female characters (or those who want to be strong) and fun, twisty plots. Although Tiffany primarily writes sci-fi, she enjoys a good story in any genre.

If she's not watching Doctor Who or putting together Star Wars Legos with her son, Tiffany is imagining what trouble her characters can get into next. She's a coffee-fueled writer of science fiction who believes challenge and opportunity can be empowering. She's trying to make the world a better (and more fun) place, one book at a time.

Tiffany lives in Tennessee with her husband, son, and three spoiled dogs.

To connect with her, visit:

tmcatron.com

Amazon Author Page: amazon.com/author/tmcatron

Facebook: facebook.com/authortmcatron
Twitter: @tmcatron
Email: books@tmcatron.com

WHAT IS PHOENIX PRIME?

Phoenix Prime began as a Ph.D. level workshop for writers to come together to improve their craft and their businesses. However, since its creation, it has evolved into a tight-knit group of authors who encourage one another, collaborate with one another, learn together, and write together.

When you hear me mention Phoenix Prime, I'm speaking of a group of people I'm proud to know and work with. They are dedicated, supportive, and all-around fun. I'm honored to be a part of this team.